MIRKA ANDOLFO'S

UNNATURAL™

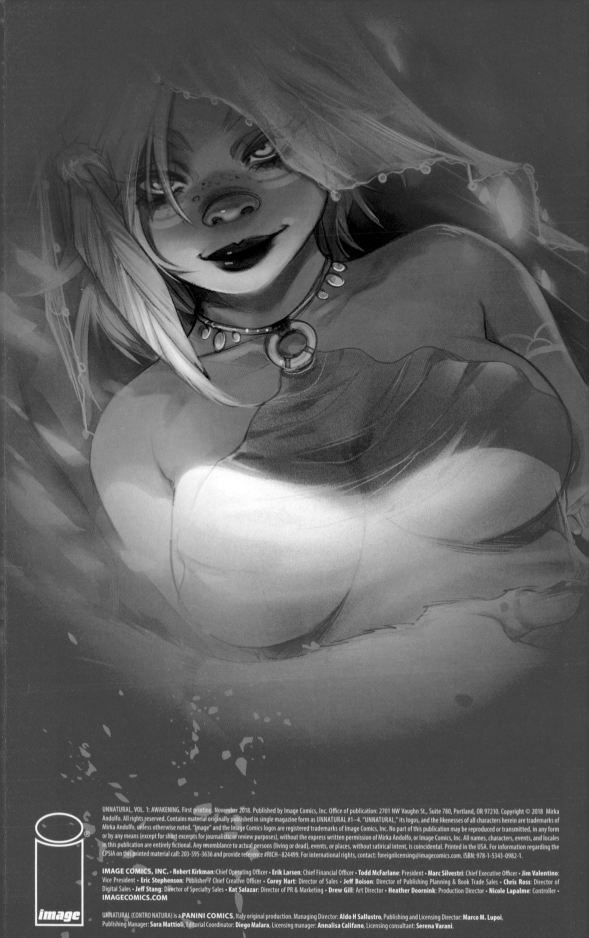

UNNATURAL, VOL. 1: AWAKENING. First printing. November 2018. Published by Image Comics, Inc. Office of publication: 2701 NW Vaughn St., Suite 780, Portland, OR 97210. Copyright © 2018 Mirka Andolfo. All rights reserved. Contains material originally published in single magazine form as UNNATURAL #1—4. "UNNATURAL," its logos, and the likenesses of all characters herein are trademarks of Mirka Andolfo, unless otherwise noted. "Image" and the Image Comics logos are registered trademarks of Image Comics, Inc. No part of this publication may be reproduced or transmitted, in any form or by any means (except for short excerpts for journalistic or review purposes), without the express written permission of Mirka Andolfo, or Image Comics, Inc. All names, characters, events, and locales in this publication are entirely fictional. Any resemblance to actual persons (living or dead), events, or places, without satirical intent, is coincidental. Printed in the USA. For information regarding the CPSIA on this printed material call: 203-595-3636 and provide reference #RICH—824499. For international rights, contact: foreignlicensing@imagecomics.com. ISBN: 978-1-5343-0982-1.

IMAGE COMICS, INC. • **Robert Kirkman**: Chief Operating Officer • **Erik Larsen**: Chief Financial Officer • **Todd McFarlane**: President • **Marc Silvestri**: Chief Executive Officer • **Jim Valentino**: Vice President • **Eric Stephenson**: Publisher / Chief Creative Officer • **Corey Hart**: Director of Sales • **Jeff Boison**: Director of Publishing Planning & Book Trade Sales • **Chris Ross**: Director of Digital Sales • **Jeff Stang**: Director of Specialty Sales • **Kat Salazar**: Director of PR & Marketing • **Drew Gill**: Art Director • **Heather Doornink**: Production Director • **Nicole Lapalme**: Controller
IMAGECOMICS.COM

UNNATURAL (CONTRO NATURA) is a **PANINI COMICS**, Italy original production. Managing Director: **Aldo H Sallustro**, Publishing and Licensing Director: **Marco M. Lupoi**, Publishing Manager: **Sara Mattioli**, Editorial Coordinator: **Diego Malara**, Licensing manager: **Annalisa Califano**, Licensing consultant: **Serena Varani**.

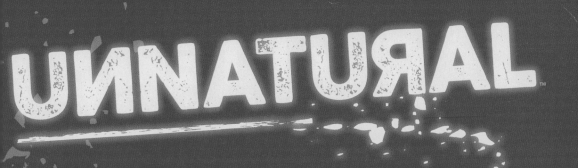

VOLUME ONE · AWAKENING

writer, artist and colorist
MIRKA ANDOLFO

colors assistant
GIANLUCA PAPI
(ARANCIA STUDIO)

lettering and production
FABIO AMELIA
(ARANCIA STUDIO)

translation from italian
ARANCIA STUDIO

cover artist
MIRKA ANDOLFO

editors
DIEGO MALARA
MARCO RICOMPENSA

design
ALESSANDRO GUCCIARDO
FABIO AMELIA

CHAPTER ONE

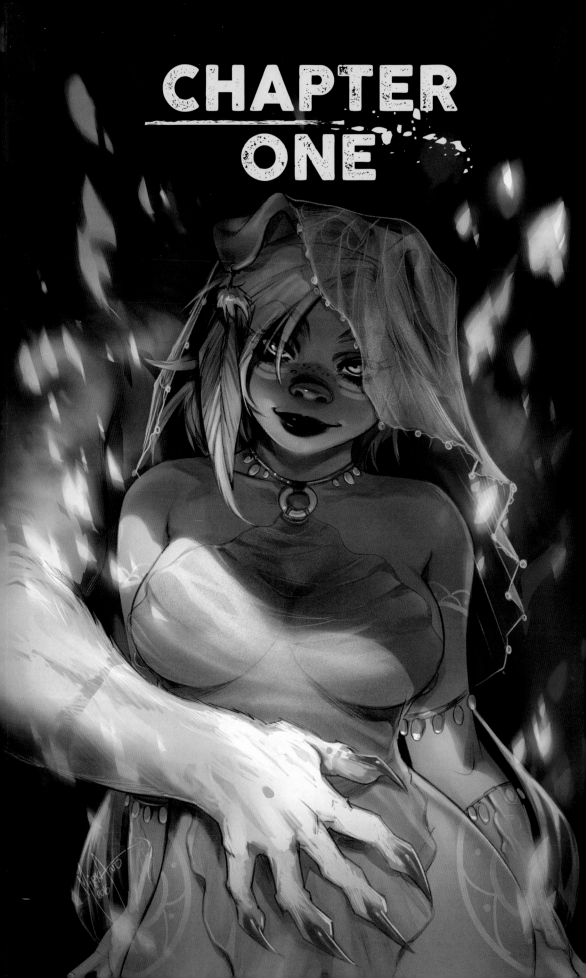

I CAN FEEL HIM...
HE'S COMING BACK TO ME...
AGAIN.
I SHOULDN'T GO FURTHER.
I KNOW THAT.

AND YET...
HEY! **EXCUSE ME!** WHAT THE **HELL** ARE YOU DOING IN THERE?!

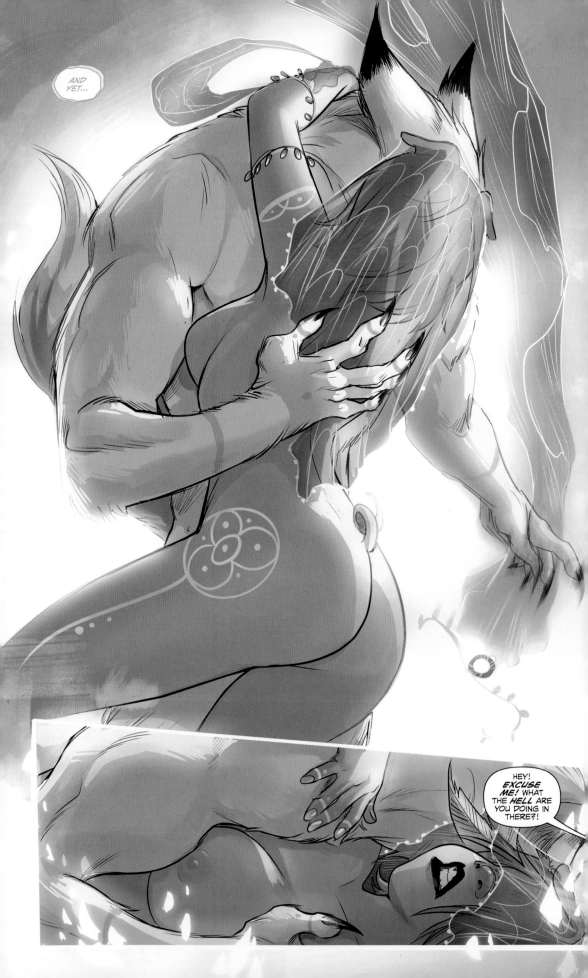

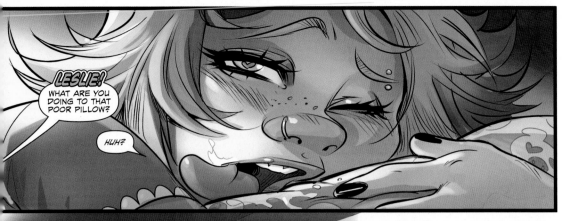

LESLIE! WHAT ARE YOU DOING TO THAT POOR PILLOW?

HUH?

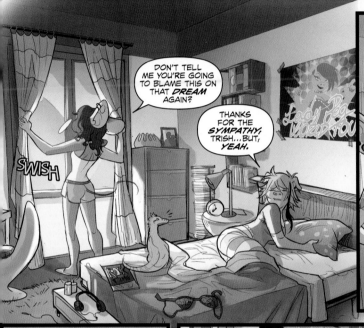

DON'T TELL ME YOU'RE GOING TO BLAME THIS ON THAT *DREAM* AGAIN?

THANKS FOR THE *SYMPATHY*, TRISH...BUT, *YEAH.*

SWISH

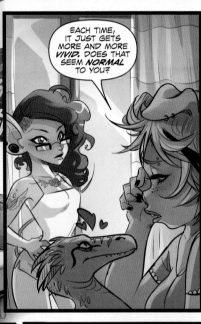

EACH TIME, IT JUST GETS MORE AND MORE *VIVID.* DOES THAT SEEM *NORMAL* TO YOU?

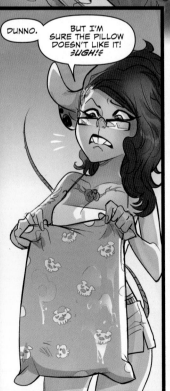

DUNNO.

BUT I'M SURE THE PILLOW DOESN'T LIKE IT! ≥UGH!≤

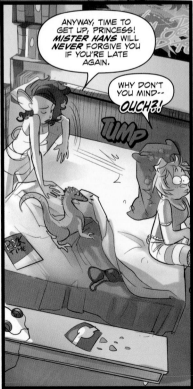

ANYWAY, TIME TO GET UP, PRINCESS! *MISTER HANS* WILL *NEVER* FORGIVE YOU IF YOU'RE LATE AGAIN.

WHY DON'T YOU MIND-- OUCH?!

TUMP

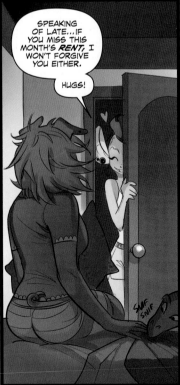

SPEAKING OF LATE...IF YOU MISS THIS MONTH'S *RENT*, I WON'T FORGIVE YOU EITHER.

HUGS!

SNIF SNIF

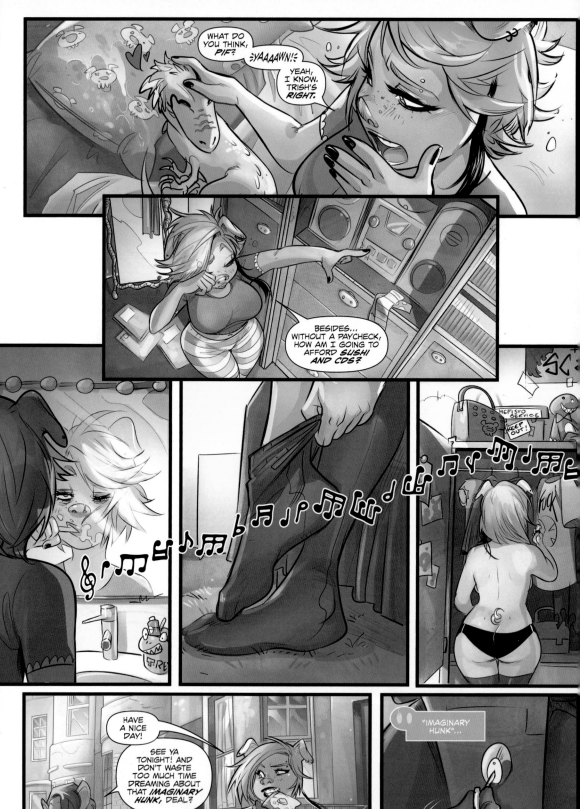

WHAT DO YOU THINK, *PIF*? ₹YAAAAWN!₹

YEAH, I KNOW. *TRISH'S* RIGHT.

BESIDES... WITHOUT A PAYCHECK, HOW AM I GOING TO AFFORD *SUSHI* AND *CDS?*

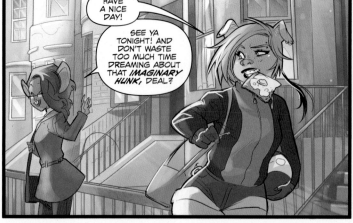

HAVE A NICE DAY!

SEE YA TONIGHT! AND DON'T WASTE TOO MUCH TIME DREAMING ABOUT THAT *IMAGINARY HUNK,* DEAL?

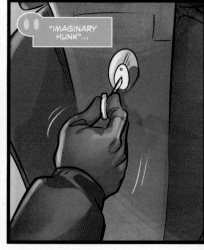

"IMAGINARY HUNK"...

TRISH'S JOKING, BUT I'M WORRIED...
THAT STUPID DREAM'S BEEN HAUNTING ME FOR A MONTH NOW. BUT LAST NIGHT WAS PARTICULARLY INTENSE.
TRADITIONAL FAMILIES: LEGAL AND SANE.
CAN'T MARRY BEFORE 25? LET THE REPRODUCTION PROGRAM HELP!
IT'S ALL SO... WRONG. WHAT'S HAPPENING TO ME?
MAYBE I JUST NEED A MAN? IT'S BEEN A WHILE...OKAY, MORE THAN A WHILE.
A HYBRID FANTASY. OH MAN, I HOPE IT PASSES. I'M NOT LOOKING TO BREAK THE LAW OR ANYTHING.
AM I ASKING FOR TOO MUCH? A NORMAL LIFE WOULD BE NICE, WITHOUT WAKING UP TO A DROOL-SOAKED PILLOW ALL FIRED UP ABOUT ILLEGAL LOVE...
MARRY WITHIN TWO DECADES AND THE STATE WILL GET YOU PAID
...AT LEAST NOT ON MY BIRTHDAY.

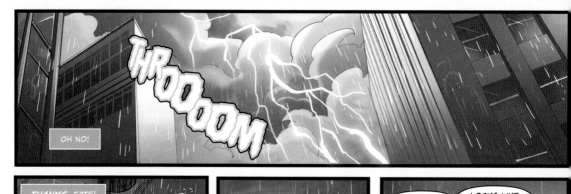

THROOOOM

OH NO!

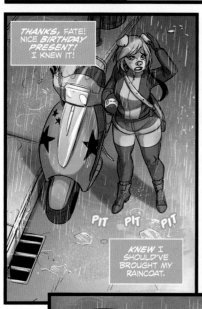

THANKS, FATE! NICE *BIRTHDAY PRESENT!* I KNEW IT!

KNEW I SHOULD'VE BROUGHT MY *RAINCOAT.*

PIT PIT PIT

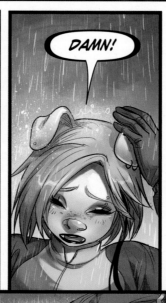

DAMN!

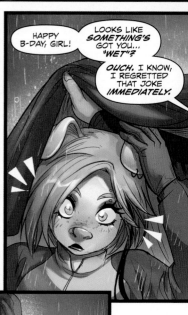

HAPPY B-DAY, GIRL!

LOOKS LIKE *SOMETHING'S* GOT YOU... *"WET"?*

OUCH. I KNOW, I REGRETTED THAT JOKE *IMMEDIATELY.*

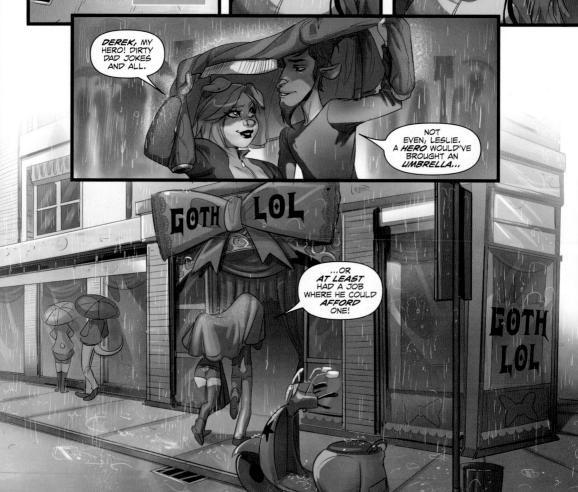

DEREK, MY *HERO!* DIRTY DAD JOKES AND ALL.

NOT EVEN, *LESLIE.* A *HERO* WOULD'VE BROUGHT AN *UMBRELLA...*

GOTH LOL

...OR *AT LEAST* HAD A JOB WHERE HE COULD *AFFORD* ONE!

GOTH LOL

THE INSTINCT OF SELF-PRESERVATION BEGINS IN THE CRADLE.
IT HELPS US. GUIDES US. SHOWS US THE RIGHT DECISIONS TO KEEP OURSELVES AND OUR PARTNERS ALIVE.
BUT SOMETIMES, WE STOP LISTENING TO ITS GUIDANCE. SOMETHING GETS IN THE WAY, AND WE START MAKING THE WRONG CHOICES. IMMORAL CHOICES.
UNNATURAL CHOICES.
WHEN THAT HAPPENS, WE COULD USE SOME HELP TO GET BACK ON THE RIGHTEOUS PATH.
THAT'S WHY THE GOVERNMENT GAVE US THE REPRODUCTION PROGRAM.
EVERYBODY KNOWS THAT HYBRIDS BETWEEN DIFFERENT SPECIES AREN'T CONCEIVED IN NATURE.
HOWEVER...

...SOME MISGUIDED TYPES START UNSUITABLE RELATIONSHIPS BETWEEN ANIMALS OF OTHER SPECIES.
OR WORSE... OF THE SAME SEX! GROSS! SO SHAMELESS AND PERVERSE!
THANKFULLY, THE GOVERNMENT HAS OUR BEST INTERESTS AT HEART.
INTRODUCING "REAL LOVE!" THE REVOLUTIONARY APP THAT KNOWS YOU BETTER THAN YOU KNOW YOURSELF!
RealLove
RealLove
REAL LOVE KNOWS WHAT YOU LIKE, AND USES THAT TO FORECAST YOUR PROCREATIVE COMPATIBILITY WITH YOUR PERFECT SAME-SPECIES PARTNER!
"BUT," YOU MAY ASK, "DO WE HAVE TO USE IT?"
SURE! AFTER ALL, IT'S YOUR DUTY. WE ALL HAVE AN OBLIGATION TO PRESERVE OUR CIVILIZATION FOR THE FUTURE. AND TO DO THAT? WE NEED REAL LOVE.
THAT'S WHY THERE'S CONSIDERABLE BONUSES FOR SUITABLE TRADITIONAL COUPLES AND HEAVY BUT FAIR SANCTIONS FOR UNSUITABLE COUPLES.
BUT DON'T WORRY! ALL ANIMALS ARE THE SAME. EVERYTHING IS BEAUTIFUL, AND A ROSY FUTURE AWAITS US!
JUST DON'T BREAK THE LAW.
CLICK

PLEASE, FOLKS. RELAX! DON'T ALL RUSH IN TO WORK AT ONCE!
EVERYONE COMFORTABLE? NEED ANYTHING? MAYBE SOME WARM MILK? OH WAIT, THAT'S RIGHT. YOU WORK FOR ME...
LET'S GET A FUCKING MOVE ON!
AND I DON'T WANT TO HEAR A WORD ABOUT THE NEW UNIFORMS, UNLESS YOU'RE HUNGRY FOR A PINK SLIP.
AHEM... MR. HANS... ABOUT THOSE NEW UNIFORMS. THEY'RE--
FOR THE CLIENTS' PLEASURE, LESLIE. NOT YOURS.
I--I KNOW... AND I'M EMBARRASSED TO EVEN SAY IT, BUT... IT'S JUST THAT...
IT'S NOT MY SIZE! FORGET WORKING IN THIS THING, I CAN'T WALK IN IT!
HE HE HE! SAUSAGES DON'T FIT INTO UNIFORMS!
SHUT UP AND GET BACK TO WORK!
LISTEN, SWEETIE. IT KILLS ME TO BE THE ONE TO TELL YOU THIS... I HATE IT, BUT THESE ARE BRAND NEW, EXPENSIVE UNIFORMS, SO IF IT DOESN'T FIT...
LOSE SOME WEIGHT, OK?!
RIGHT, BUT... WHAT ABOUT TODAY?

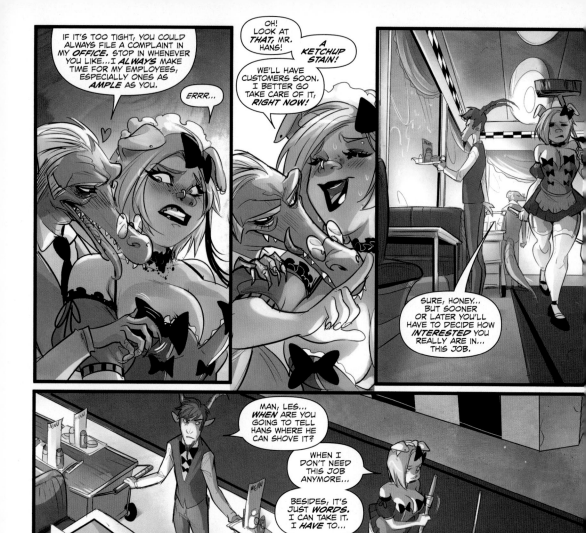

IF IT'S TOO TIGHT, YOU COULD ALWAYS FILE A COMPLAINT IN MY *OFFICE*. STOP IN WHENEVER YOU LIKE... I *ALWAYS* MAKE TIME FOR MY EMPLOYEES, ESPECIALLY ONES AS *AMPLE* AS YOU.

ERRR...

OH! LOOK AT *THAT*, MR. HANS!

A KETCHUP STAIN!

WE'LL HAVE CUSTOMERS SOON. I BETTER GO TAKE CARE OF IT, *RIGHT NOW!*

SURE, HONEY... BUT SOONER OR LATER YOU'LL HAVE TO DECIDE HOW *INTERESTED* YOU REALLY ARE IN... THIS JOB.

MAN, LES... *WHEN* ARE YOU GOING TO TELL HANS WHERE HE CAN SHOVE IT?

WHEN I DON'T NEED THIS JOB ANYMORE...

BESIDES, IT'S JUST *WORDS.* I CAN TAKE IT. I *HAVE* TO...

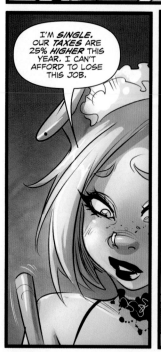

I'M *SINGLE.* OUR *TAXES* ARE 25% *HIGHER* THIS YEAR. I CAN'T AFFORD TO LOSE THIS JOB.

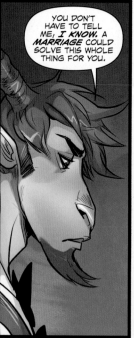

YOU DON'T HAVE TO TELL ME, I *KNOW.* A *MARRIAGE* COULD SOLVE THIS WHOLE THING FOR YOU.

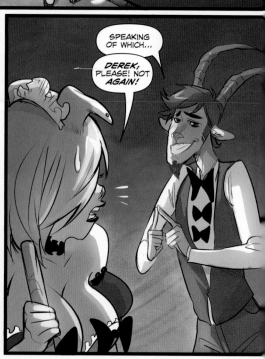

SPEAKING OF WHICH...

DEREK, PLEASE! NOT *AGAIN!*

LOOK AT THIS HUNK!
HE'S YOUR SPECIES, HANDSOME, EDUCATED, ELEGANT AND HAS EXCELLENT TEETH...TOGETHER YOU'D BE PERFECT!
WHAT'S HOLDING YOU BACK?
MAYBE, AND JUST GO WITH ME HERE...BECAUSE THAT'S MAX, YOUR BOYFRIEND?
AND, YOU KNOW, WE'D GO TO JAIL IF PEOPLE FIGURED IT OUT!
...BUT IF THEY DIDN'T, WE'D BE RICH, LES! AND NO MORE SINGLES TAXES!
JUST THINK, IF YOU GUYS HAVE A BABY...
DO YOU REALIZE WHAT YOU'RE ASKING ME, DEREK?
SDENG
OF COURSE I DO! YOU'RE MY BEST FRIEND, LES. IF MAX DOESN'T FIND A "SUITABLE PARTNER" THEY'LL MAKE HIM DO THAT STUPID PROCREATION PROGRAM. THEY'LL FORCE HIM TO FIND SOMEONE HE CAN'T STAND, OF HIS SPECIES, OR THEY'LL TAX US SO MUCH WE'LL BE OUT ON THE STREET!
SHHH! ARE YOU INSANE?! DO YOU WANT THEM TO HEAR US?
AT LEAST IF IT WAS YOU, WE COULD BE COMFORT-ABLE!
DEREK, I'M SORRY.
IT'S TOO RISKY. YOU KNOW THAT...
AND HAVE YOU EVER STOPPED TO CONSIDER THAT MAYBE THERE'S A REASON THE LAWS ARE WHAT THEY ARE?

YOU KNOW I LOVE YOU, AND I UNDERSTAND YOUR SITUATION.
BUT IT'S NOT UP TO ME TO DECIDE WHAT'S LEGAL AND WHAT'S NOT...
YEAH. WHAT'S "UNNATURAL," RIGHT?
FUNNY... AREN'T YOUR DREAMS ILLEGAL THEN?
STOOOP! NON-REQUESTED (AND NOT AUTHORIZED) BREAK ENDS NOW!
LISTEN, LESLIE...
STOP, DEREK. I'M FED UP.
YOU, MR. HANS, THE GOVERNMENT. IT DOESN'T MATTER WHY. YOU'RE ALL DOING THE SAME THING...
TELLING ME WHAT TO DO.

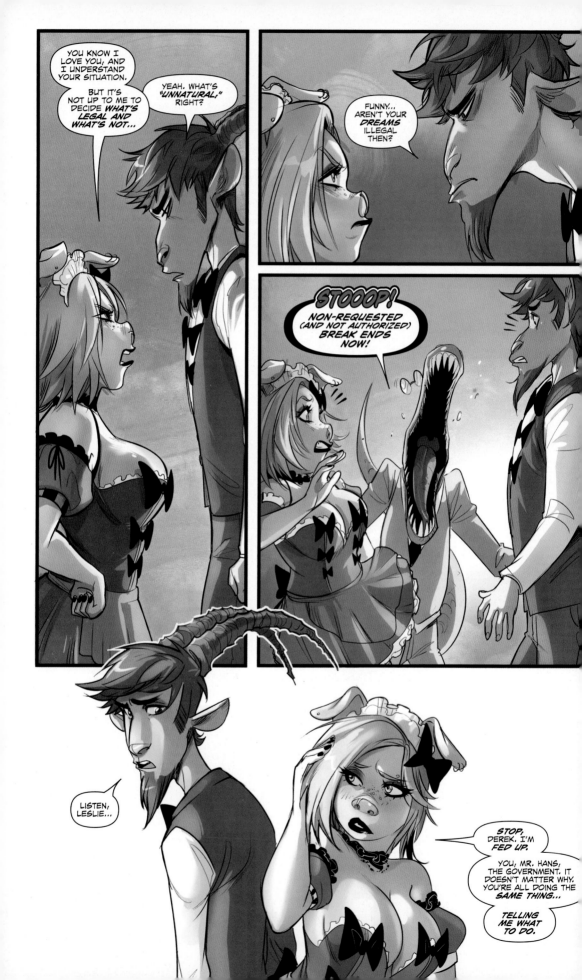

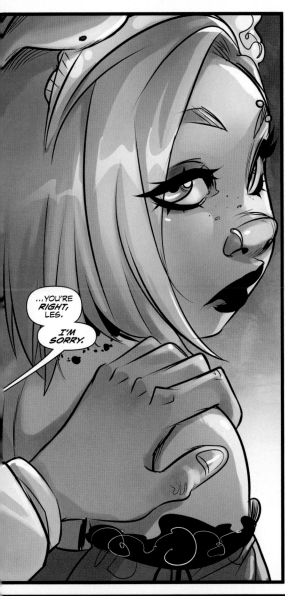

...YOU'RE *RIGHT*, LES.

I'M SORRY.

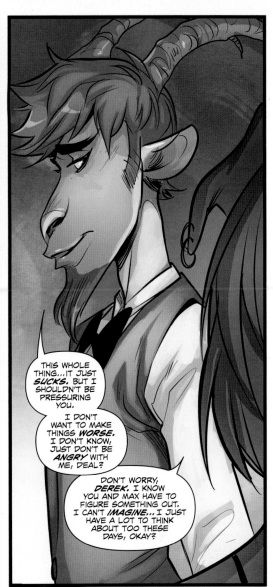

THIS WHOLE THING...IT JUST *SUCKS.* BUT I SHOULDN'T BE PRESSURING YOU.

I DON'T WANT TO MAKE THINGS *WORSE.* I DON'T KNOW, JUST DON'T BE *ANGRY* WITH ME, DEAL?

DON'T WORRY, *DEREK.* I KNOW YOU AND MAX HAVE TO FIGURE SOMETHING OUT. I CAN'T *IMAGINE*... I JUST HAVE A LOT TO THINK ABOUT TOO THESE DAYS, OKAY?

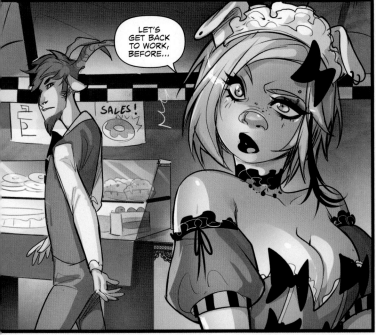

LET'S GET BACK TO WORK, BEFORE...

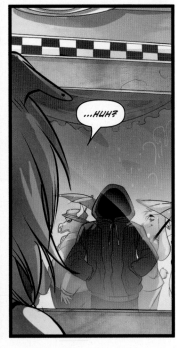

...HUH?

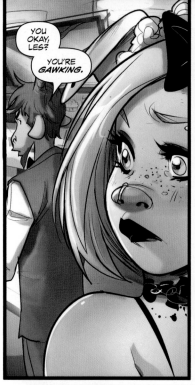

YOU OKAY, LES? YOU'RE *GAWKING.*

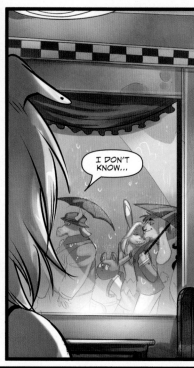

I DON'T KNOW...

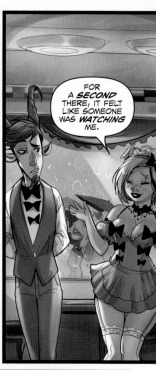

FOR A *SECOND* THERE, IT FELT LIKE SOMEONE WAS *WATCHING* ME.

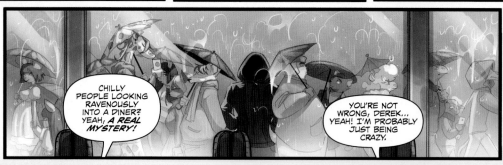

CHILLY PEOPLE LOOKING RAVENOUSLY INTO A DINER? YEAH, *A REAL MYSTERY!*

YOU'RE NOT WRONG, DEREK... YEAH! I'M PROBABLY JUST BEING CRAZY.

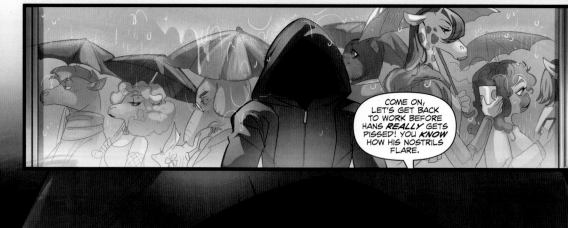

COME ON, LET'S GET BACK TO WORK BEFORE HANS *REALLY* GETS PISSED! YOU *KNOW* HOW HIS NOSTRILS FLARE.

CAN'T IMAGINE ANYTHING *WORSE* THAN THAT...

...e Shift Later.
AAH... FINALLY!
IF PARADISE EXISTED, THIS WOULD BE IT.
WELL, OKAY... MAYBE THERE'D BE SOME CHEESECAKE THERE...
...AND SOME SUSHI...
GOOD THING BACK IN THE REAL WORLD, WE'VE GOT WINE... ENOUGH TO MAKE ME SERIOUSLY CONSIDER DEREK'S PROPOSAL.
THE REPRODUCTION PROGRAM...
IT ALWAYS BRINGS UP BAD MEMORIES.
SINCE I WAS BORN, I'VE BEEN TOLD TO FIND A PARTNER! PROCREATE! BUT THERE'S MORE TO LIFE THAN THAT! I DON'T EVEN KNOW IF I WANT TO FALL IN LOVE...
WITH WHAT MAX AND DEREK ARE ASKING...AT LEAST I'D BE MAKING MY OWN CHOICE. AND THEY'D BE HAPPY.

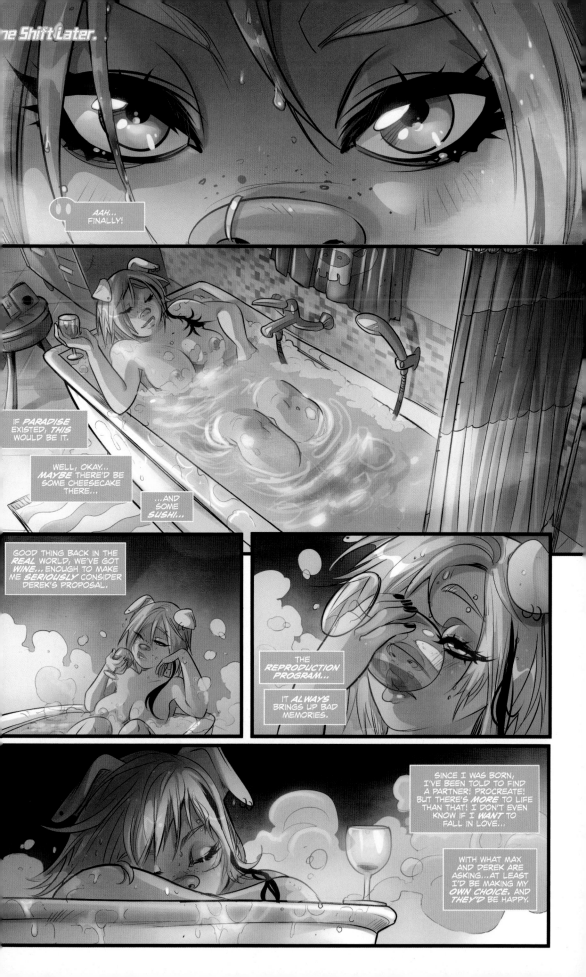

BUT STILL, TO MYSELF...I HAVE TO ADMIT, SECRETLY...
...IF I DID HAVE TO CHOOSE SOMEONE... THE CHOICE WOULD BE...
...UNNATURAL...
I'D CHOOSE HIM.
THE WOLF OF MY DREAMS.

IS SOMETHING WRONG WITH ME? I HAVE SUCH DIRTY THOUGHTS, SO MANY OF THEM, BUT...
WE'RE OF DIFFERENT SPECIES; WE CAN'T HAVE CHILDREN.
THIS IS WRONG! IT SAYS SO ON TV!
AND YET... IT FEELS SO GOOD.
MAYBE I'M OVERTHINKING THINGS.
IT'S JUST A DREAM, RIGHT?
WHAT HARM COULD IT POSSIBLY DO...TO LET MYSELF GO...IN A DREAM?

DIIIIIIIRTY...
MLLMML
TRISH!
I DIDN'T-- I WASN'T-- I MEAN--
YOU DID. YOU WERE. YOU MEANT...
TO MAKE OUT WITH THAT GLASS!
HERE. SOMETHING MORE WHOLESOME FOR YOUR MOUTH: DINNER.
SUSHI SAURO
WHAAAAT?! YOU STOPPED BY SUSHISAURO? SHUT UP!
HELL YEAH! I KNOW WHAT YOU NEED. WHAT BETTER WAY TO CELEBRATE YOUR BIRTHDAY?
OR, YOU KNOW, THE FIRST OF THE MONTH, THE END OF YOUR PERIOD, THE FIRST SUNDAY...
TAC
TAC
ALL OF THE ABOVE! THANK YOU! LET'S DIG IN!
YOU'RE WELCOME. JUST BE CAREFUL WITH THE CHOPSTICKS...
AFTER WHAT I WITNESSED WITH THAT GLASS, I DON'T WANT YOU GETTING SPLINTERS IN THE BACK OF YOUR THROAT.
HOW FUNNY.

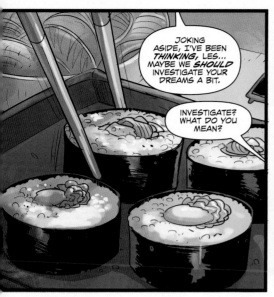

JOKING ASIDE, I'VE BEEN *THINKING*, LES... MAYBE WE *SHOULD* INVESTIGATE YOUR DREAMS A BIT.

INVESTIGATE? WHAT DO YOU MEAN?

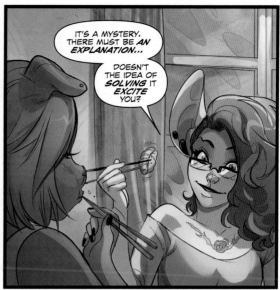

IT'S A MYSTERY. THERE MUST BE *AN EXPLANATION...*

DOESN'T THE IDEA OF *SOLVING* IT *EXCITE* YOU?

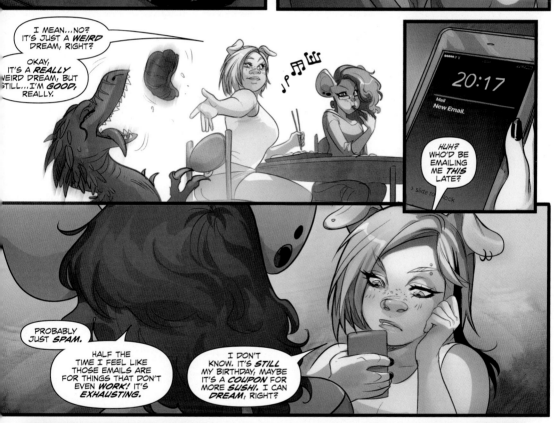

I MEAN...NO? IT'S JUST A *WEIRD* DREAM, RIGHT?

OKAY, IT'S A *REALLY* WEIRD DREAM, BUT STILL...I'M *GOOD*, REALLY.

20:17

Mail
New Email.

> slide to unlock

HUH? WHO'D BE EMAILING ME *THIS* LATE?

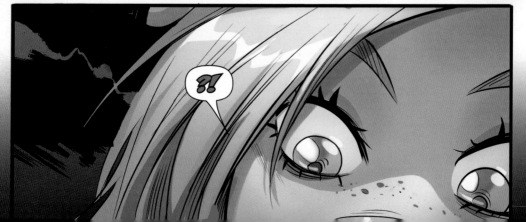

PROBABLY JUST *SPAM*.

HALF THE TIME I FEEL LIKE THOSE EMAILS ARE FOR THINGS THAT DON'T EVEN *WORK!* IT'S *EXHAUSTING*.

I DON'T KNOW. IT'S *STILL* MY BIRTHDAY, MAYBE IT'S A *COUPON* FOR MORE *SUSHI*. I CAN *DREAM*, RIGHT?

?!

LESLIE? WHAT IS IT?
THE APOCALYPSE.
LOOK.
I'VE BEEN 25 FOR A FEW HOURS, AND ALREADY I'M STUCK IN...
20:17
All Inboxes (1)
22%
From: Reproduction Program Office
To: Leslie
Reproduction Program
Now
Dear Miss Leslie J. Blair, as you know, after reaching 25 years of age, each citizen can be included in the Reproduction Program, as soon as a person of the same species with a sufficiently high procreative compatibility is found. We are happy to inform you that we have found your soul mate! The appointment is for tomorrow at 6:00PM.
THE REPRODUCTION PROGRAM!

CHAPTER
TWO
SUSHI
SAURO

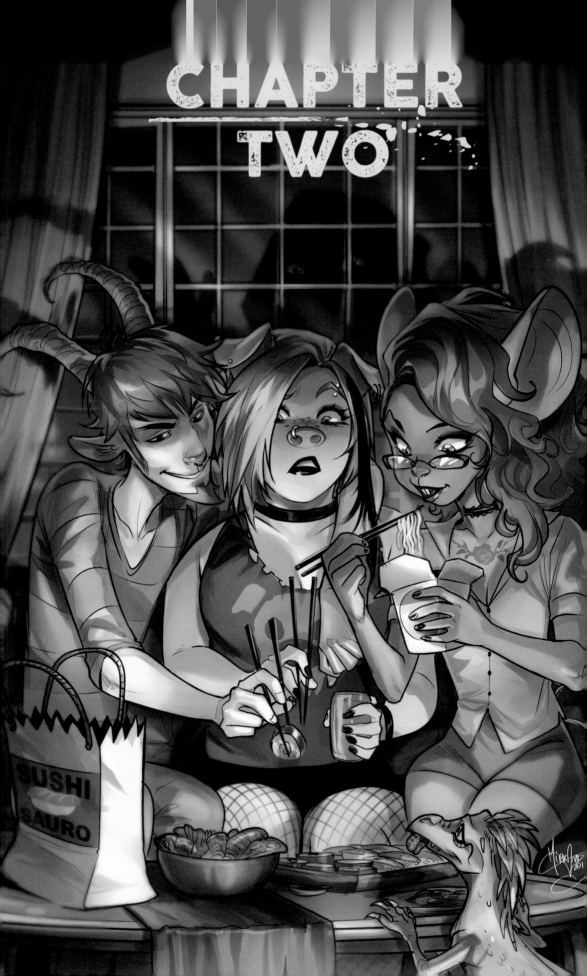

New Roark County Courthouse.
TODAY MARKS THE END OF THE INFAMOUS SINCLAIR-BOSCH TRIAL, A SCANDAL THAT'S KEPT HONEST NEW ROARKERS GLUED TO THEIR SEATS FOR MONTHS.
THE DUO'S INCONSIDERATE AND UNNATURAL ACTIONS LEFT THEM CHARGED WITH FRAUD AGAINST THE STATE AND CRIMES AGAINST THE SPECIES. NOW? THE VERDICT IS IN.
SINCLAIR AND BOSCH HAVE BEEN SENTENCED TO FIVE YEARS IN PRISON, TO BE SERVED AT ONE OF THE REPRODUCTION PROGRAM'S BEAUTIFUL DEVIANCE REHABILITATION CENTERS.
LET'S WISH THEM LUCK! THIS WAS THEIR FIRST OFFENSE, AND AS WE ALL KNOW...TWO-TIME SPECIES OFFENDERS AUTOMATICALLY FACE THE DEATH PENALTY.
AND REMEMBER, DEAR CITIZENS... ALL ANIMALS ARE EQUAL AS LONG AS THEY RESPECT THE LAW...AND NATURE!

STRONG BUT COMPASSIONATE WORDS FROM OUR LEADER TODAY AS ANOTHER SPECIES-DEVIANT COUPLE IS SENTENCED THIS MORNING.
IN THESE FRIGHTENING TIMES, IT'S IMPORTANT TO REMEMBER THAT DECENCY LAWS, THOUGH THEY MAY SEEM HARSH, ARE FOR OUR OWN PROTECTION.
DISGUSTING!
WAIT! IT'S SINCLAIR AND BOSCH! THE TWO DEVIANTS ARE EXITING THE COURTHOUSE NOW, ESCORTED BY LOCAL LAW ENFORCEMENT...
YOU TWO! DANA MUHTON, RNN NEWS.
TELL ME, WHAT IS YOUR REACTION TO THE SENTENCE? CAN YOU EVER TRULY RETURN TO A HEALTHY, MORAL LIFESTYLE AFTER WHAT YOU'VE DONE?
PERVERTS! THEY'LL NEVER CHANGE!
FREE BOSCH AND SINCLAIR!
THEY CAN'T CHANGE! SEND 'EM TO THE SLAUGHTERHOUSE!
YOU WANT TO KNOW WHAT I THINK, DANA? YOUR MORALS ARE OUT OF DATE. YOU THINK WE'RE DONE? WE'RE FIGHTING THIS VERDICT!
FUCK THE SLAUGHTERHOUSE AND FUCK THE LEADER!
FREEDOM = CHOICE
YOU CALL IT DEVIANCY, WE CALL IT LOVE!
DAMN RIGHT! DOWN WITH THE FUCKING LEADER!
THAT'S ENOUGH, FREAK!
FREEDOM = CHOICE
TUNK
YOU CALL IT DEVIANCY, WE CALL IT LOVE!
YES
FREE LOVE
ACTION ON THE STREETS AS WHAT AGAIN APPEAR TO BE PROFESSIONAL PROTESTORS OBSTRUCT THE PEACEFUL COURSE OF JUSTICE!

GET THAT CAMERA OUT OF HERE!
LOOKS LIKE WE'LL HAVE TO TAKE A BREAK. STAY WITH US, THIS IS DANA MUHTON WITH RNN NEWS...
Lady Peg tour
LES! YOU AWAKE? WHAT ARE YOU WATCHING?
...NOTHING, TRISH. I'M JUST... IN A TRANCE, FEELS LIKE. COULDN'T SLEEP AT ALL LAST NIGHT.
I CAN TELL! YOUR PILLOW'S DRY.
COME ON, SHUT THAT OFF. THE NEWS'LL RUIN YOUR APPETITE, AND THIS BREAKFAST IS ON POINT.
YOU'VE GOT TO GET OUT OF BED EVENTUALLY, LES.
OINK
...I'M GOOD, TRISH. THANKS.
WHAT, IT'S SUSHI OR NOTHING FOR YOU NOW?
IT'S NOT THAT...I'M JUST NOT HUNGRY, THAT'S ALL.
YOU'RE NOT HUNGRY? YOU?!
OKAY. SOMETHING'S UP WITH YOU, LESLIE, AND NOW I KNOW IT'S SERIOUS.
PURRR

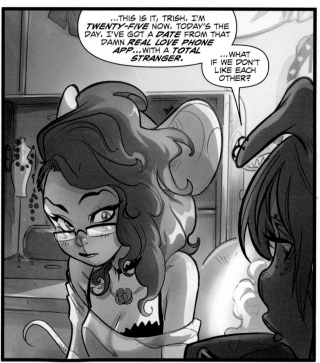

...THIS IS IT, TRISH. I'M *TWENTY-FIVE* NOW. TODAY'S THE DAY. I'VE GOT A *DATE* FROM THAT DAMN *REAL LOVE PHONE APP*...WITH A *TOTAL STRANGER.*

...WHAT IF WE DON'T LIKE EACH OTHER?

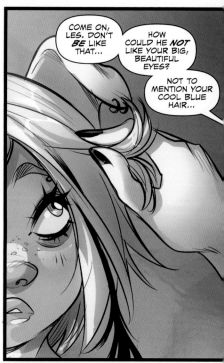

COME ON, LES. DON'T *BE* LIKE THAT...

HOW COULD HE *NOT* LIKE YOUR *BIG, BEAUTIFUL* EYES?

NOT TO MENTION YOUR *COOL BLUE* HAIR...

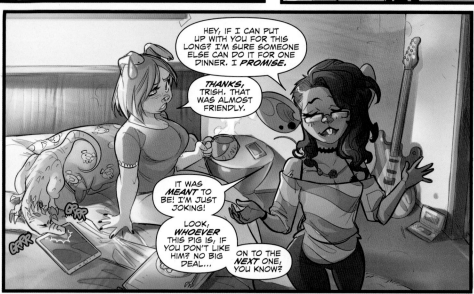

HEY, IF I CAN PUT UP WITH YOU FOR THIS LONG? I'M SURE SOMEONE ELSE CAN DO IT FOR ONE DINNER. I *PROMISE.*

THANKS, TRISH. THAT WAS ALMOST FRIENDLY.

IT WAS *MEANT* TO BE! I'M JUST JOKING!

LOOK, *WHOEVER* THIS PIG IS, IF YOU DON'T LIKE HIM? NO BIG DEAL...

ON TO THE *NEXT* ONE, YOU KNOW?

BRRR

BRRR

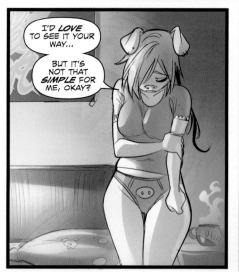

I'D *LOVE* TO SEE IT YOUR WAY...

BUT IT'S NOT THAT *SIMPLE* FOR ME, OKAY?

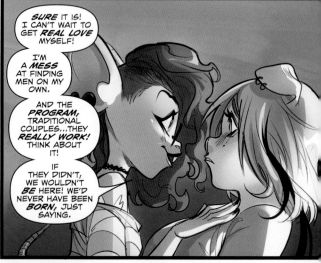

SURE IT IS! I CAN'T WAIT TO GET *REAL LOVE* MYSELF!

I'M A *MESS* AT FINDING MEN ON MY OWN.

AND THE *PROGRAM,* TRADITIONAL COUPLES...THEY *REALLY WORK!* THINK ABOUT IT!

IF THEY DIDN'T, WE WOULDN'T *BE* HERE! WE'D NEVER HAVE BEEN *BORN,* JUST SAYING.

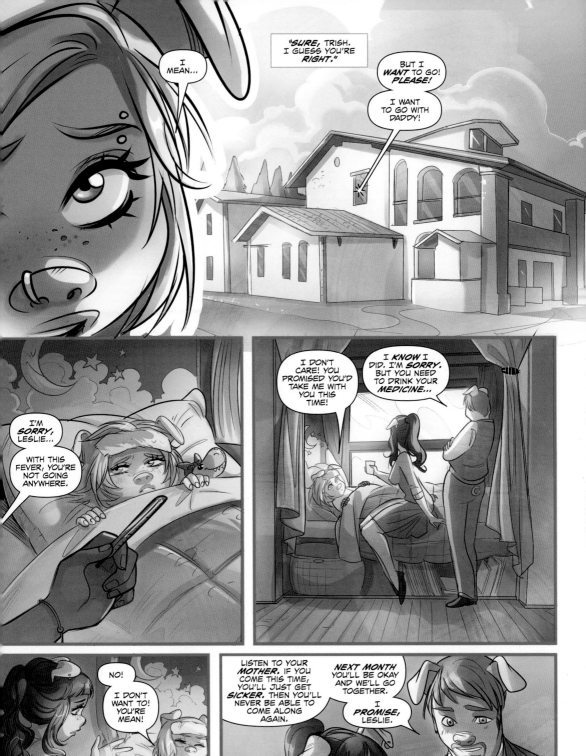

"SURE, TRISH. I GUESS YOU'RE RIGHT."

I MEAN...

BUT I WANT TO GO! PLEASE!

I WANT TO GO WITH DADDY!

I DON'T CARE! YOU PROMISED YOU'D TAKE ME WITH YOU THIS TIME!

I KNOW I DID. I'M SORRY. BUT YOU NEED TO DRINK YOUR MEDICINE...

I'M SORRY, LESLIE...

WITH THIS FEVER, YOU'RE NOT GOING ANYWHERE.

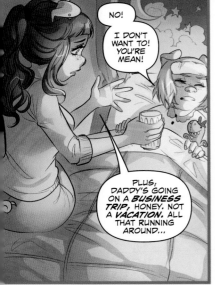

NO!

I DON'T WANT TO! YOU'RE MEAN!

PLUS, DADDY'S GOING ON A BUSINESS TRIP, HONEY. NOT A VACATION. ALL THAT RUNNING AROUND...

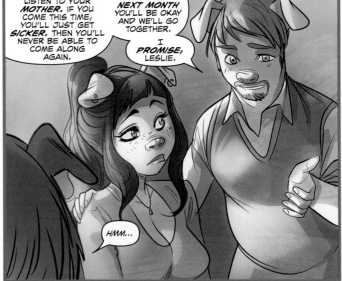

LISTEN TO YOUR MOTHER. IF YOU COME THIS TIME, YOU'LL JUST GET SICKER. THEN YOU'LL NEVER BE ABLE TO COME ALONG AGAIN.

NEXT MONTH YOU'LL BE OKAY AND WE'LL GO TOGETHER.

I PROMISE, LESLIE.

HMM...

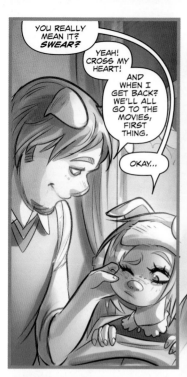

YOU REALLY MEAN IT? *SWEAR?*

YEAH! CROSS MY HEART!

AND WHEN I GET BACK? WE'LL ALL GO TO THE MOVIES, FIRST THING.

OKAY...

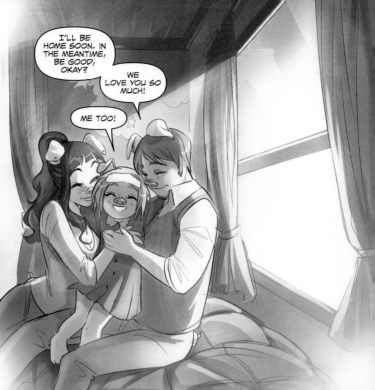

I'LL BE HOME SOON. IN THE MEANTIME, BE GOOD, OKAY?

WE LOVE YOU SO MUCH!

ME TOO!

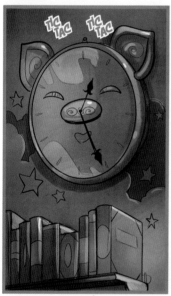

TIC TAC   TIC TAC

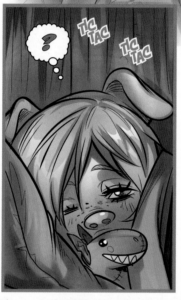

?   TIC TAC

TIC TAC

TIC TAC

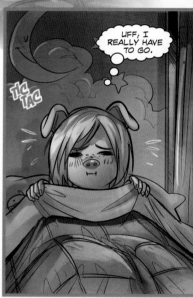

UFF, I REALLY HAVE TO GO.

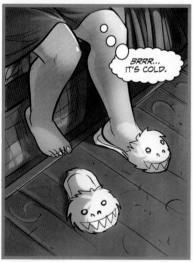

BRRR... IT'S COLD.

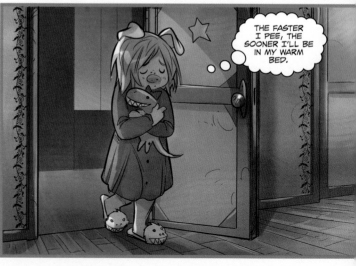

THE FASTER I PEE, THE SOONER I'LL BE IN MY WARM BED.

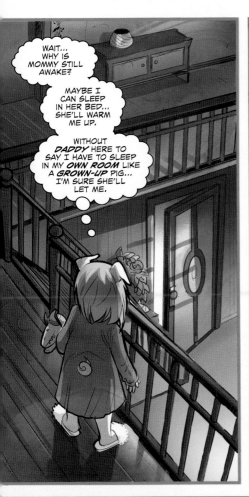

WAIT... WHY IS MOMMY STILL AWAKE?

MAYBE I CAN SLEEP IN HER BED... SHE'LL WARM ME UP.

WITHOUT *DADDY* HERE TO SAY I HAVE TO SLEEP IN MY *OWN ROOM* LIKE A *GROWN-UP* PIG... I'M SURE SHE'LL LET ME.

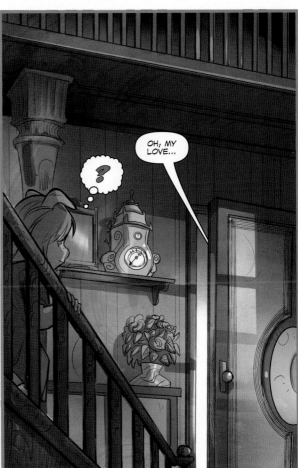

?

OH, MY LOVE...

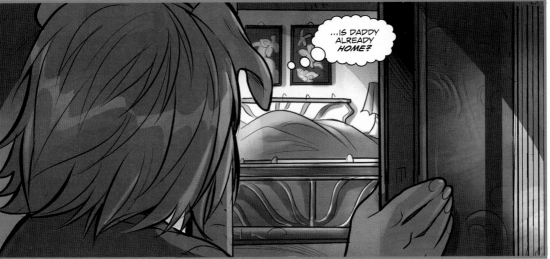

...IS DADDY ALREADY *HOME?*

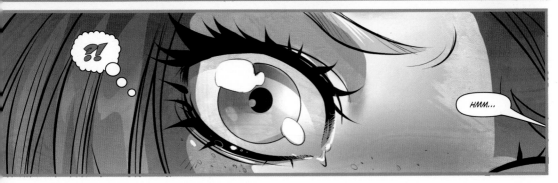

?!

HMM...

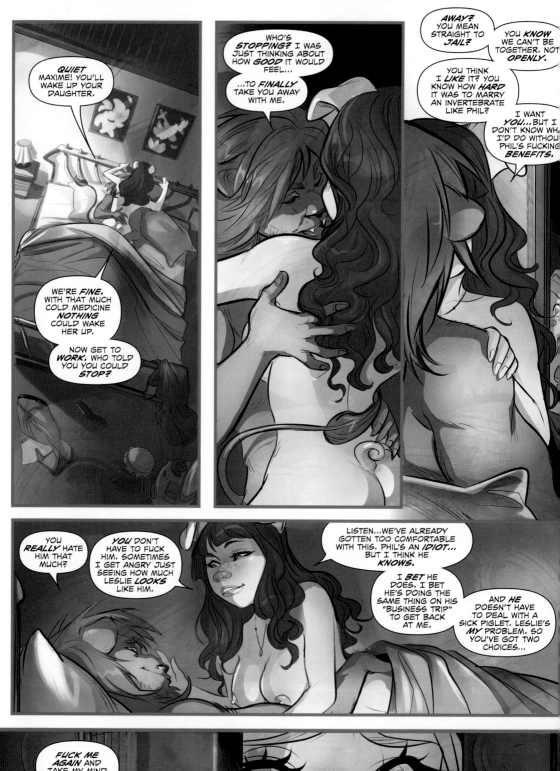

QUIET. MAXIME! YOU'LL WAKE UP YOUR DAUGHTER.

WE'RE FINE. WITH THAT MUCH COLD MEDICINE NOTHING COULD WAKE HER UP.

NOW GET TO WORK. WHO TOLD YOU YOU COULD STOP?

WHO'S STOPPING? I WAS JUST THINKING ABOUT HOW GOOD IT WOULD FEEL...

...TO FINALLY TAKE YOU AWAY WITH ME.

AWAY? YOU MEAN STRAIGHT TO JAIL?

YOU KNOW WE CAN'T BE TOGETHER. NOT OPENLY.

YOU THINK I LIKE IT? YOU KNOW HOW HARD IT WAS TO MARRY AN INVERTEBRATE LIKE PHIL?

I WANT YOU...BUT I DON'T KNOW WH. I'D DO WITHOUT PHIL'S FUCKING BENEFITS.

YOU REALLY HATE HIM THAT MUCH?

YOU DON'T HAVE TO FUCK HIM. SOMETIMES I GET ANGRY JUST SEEING HOW MUCH LESLIE LOOKS LIKE HIM.

LISTEN...WE'VE ALREADY GOTTEN TOO COMFORTABLE WITH THIS. PHIL'S AN IDIOT... BUT I THINK HE KNOWS.

I BET HE DOES. I BET HE'S DOING THE SAME THING ON HIS "BUSINESS TRIP" TO GET BACK AT ME.

AND HE DOESN'T HAVE TO DEAL WITH A SICK PIGLET. LESLIE'S MY PROBLEM. SO YOU'VE GOT TWO CHOICES...

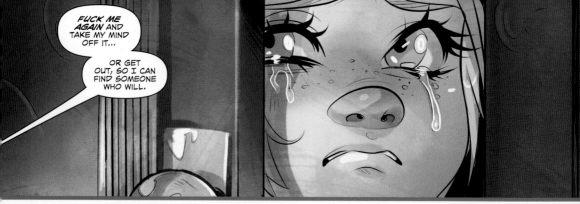

FUCK ME AGAIN AND TAKE MY MIND OFF IT...

OR GET OUT, SO I CAN FIND SOMEONE WHO WILL.

ARRANGED SAME-SPECIES MARRIAGES DON'T ALWAYS GO WELL, TRISH.
I DON'T WANT THAT TO BE ME...
IT'S NOT ALWAYS LIKE THAT, LES.
I USED TO BE A REBEL TOO, WHEN I WAS YOUNGER...BUT THE REPRODUCTION PROGRAM IS GOOD. IF YOU'D TRIED MORE WHEN YOU WERE OUT WITH ME AND DEREK, MAYBE YOU WOULDN'T HAVE NEEDED IT AT ALL.
THAT IS NOT HELPFUL RIGHT NOW.
I'M JUST SAYING...WE ALL NEED TO OWN OUR CHOICES. IF YOU'D FOUND A PARTNER FROM YOUR SPECIES BEFORE YOU WERE TWENTY-FIVE, THE STATE WOULDN'T HAVE TO.
YOU NEED TO ACCEPT IT OR YOU'LL NEVER BE HAPPY. DEREK SHOULD TOO...
IT'S JUST...SO BIG, TRISH. I'M...I'M SCARED.
PURRRRR
SCARED? YOU YOU DON'T HAVE TO BE SCARED, LES. JUST BECAUSE I'M REALISTIC ABOUT YOUR SITUATION DOESN'T MEAN I DON'T WANT THE BEST FOR YOU.
IF YOU MEET AN IDIOT? I'LL BE THERE TO PUT MY FOOT UP HIS ASS. IT'LL WORK OUT, LES. IT REALLY WILL.
PURR
THANKS, TRISH.

OKAY. IF WE'RE GOING TO DO THIS? LET'S *DO* THIS. LIKE RIPPING OFF A *BAND-AID.*
I'LL MEET HIM SOON ENOUGH, BUT LET'S CHEAT AHEAD AND SEE WHO *REAL LOVE'S* FOUND FOR *ME...*
PLEASE BE HOT, PLEASE BE HOT, PLEASE BE HOT...
RealLove
CLICK
WHAT? NO PICS?!
HE MUST BE HORRIBLE...
BUT HEY! LOOK! SEEMS LIKE HE'S GOT A LOT IN *COMMON* WITH YOU.
NICHOLAS JONES
add friend follow message
Interested in
Sushi
Music
Photos
no photo
NICHOLAS JONES
I Love Sushi!!! Would eat it every day if I could!
Like Comment Share
40 Likes
NICHOLAS JONES
Music is probably my biggest passion!
Like Comment Share
32 Likes
NICHOLAS JONES
I like big, beautiful pigs!
Like Comment Share
138 Likes
I BET HE'S GOOD IN *BED* TOO. THE TYPE THAT'LL MAKE YOU FORGET ALL YOUR SCANDALOUS *WOLF* DREAMS.
YOU *NAUGHTY GIRL.*
STOP IT! YOU KNOW IT'S EMBARRASSING... I CAN'T *HELP* HAVING THEM!
SO YOU'VE GOT A WEIRD RECURRING SEX DREAM THAT LEAVES YOU DROOLING THROUGH YOUR SHEETS AND I'M NOT ALLOWED TO *JOKE* ABOUT IT?
MAYBE IT'S YOUR *SUBCONSCIOUS* SPEAKING TO YOU, LES.
AND SAYING WHAT...THAT I SHOULD ONLY SLEEP WITH PEOPLE WHO'LL LAND ME IN *JAIL?*
I DON'T KNOW.
MAYBE IT'S TIME YOU ASKED A *PROFESSIONAL* FOR ADVICE IF YOU'RE *REALLY* ONLY INTERESTED IN *FORBIDDEN RELATION-SHIPS.*
OONK OONK
BUT MAYBE WAIT UNTIL *AFTER* THIS DATE, DEAL?
JUST GIVE IT A TRY! LOOK! YOUR *DRIVER'S* ALREADY HERE, MADAM.
YOU BETTER GO, OTHERWISE HE'LL *CHARGE* EXTRA.
CHILL OUT, TRISH. YOU KNOW IT'S *DEREK.*
MY POINT EXACTLY. NOW GET MOVING...

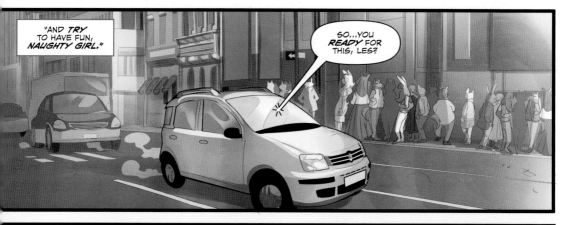

"AND *TRY* TO HAVE FUN, *NAUGHTY GIRL*."

SO...YOU *READY* FOR THIS, LES?

I MEAN... DOES IT *CHANGE* ANYTHING IF I SAY "NO"?

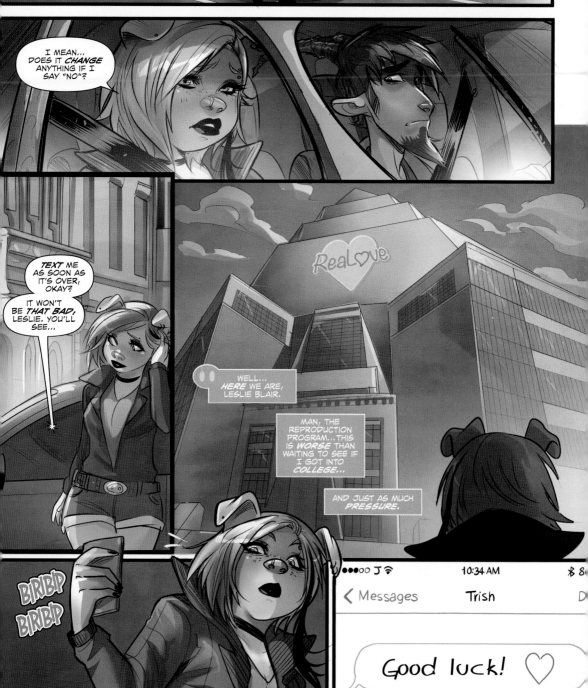

TEXT ME AS SOON AS IT'S OVER, OKAY?

IT WON'T BE *THAT BAD*, LESLIE. YOU'LL SEE...

WELL... *HERE* WE ARE, LESLIE BLAIR.

MAN, THE REPRODUCTION PROGRAM...THIS IS *WORSE* THAN WAITING TO SEE IF I GOT INTO *COLLEGE*...

AND JUST AS MUCH *PRESSURE*.

BIRIBIP BIRIBIP

●●●○○ J 📶   10:34 AM   ✳ 8

‹ Messages   Trish   D

Good luck! ♡

TRISH! THAT *BETTER* NOT STILL BE YOUR *PHONE* IN YOUR HAND...AND YOUR ON-THE-CLOCK FINGERS TYPING ON IT.

WHAT? NO! I'M JUST *WORKING*, SIR.

I'D *HOPE SO. EMAIL OUTREACH* DOESN'T WRITE ITSELF, AND I DIDN'T HIRE YOU TO PLAY *"ANGRY DINOSAURS."*

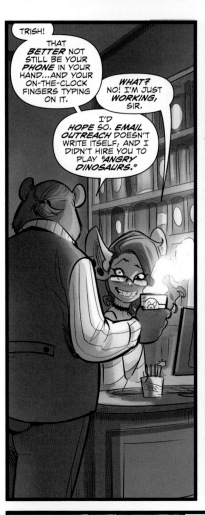

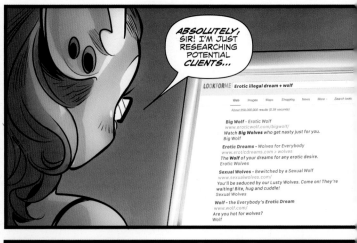

ABSOLUTELY, SIR! I'M JUST RESEARCHING POTENTIAL *CLIENTS*...

LOOKFORME Erotic illegal dream + wolf

Web Images Maps Shopping News More ▾ Search tools

About 358,000,000 results (0.26 seconds)

Big Wolf - Erotic Wolf
www.eroticwolf.com/bigwolf/
Watch **Big Wolves** who get nasty just for you.
Big Wolf

Erotic Dreams - Wolves for Everybody
www.eroticdreams.com › wolves
The **Wolf** of your dreams for any erotic desire.
Erotic Wolves

Sexual Wolves - Bewitched by a Sexual Wolf
www.sexualwolves.com/
You'll be seduced by our Lusty Wolves. Come on! They're waiting! Bite, hug and cuddle!
Sexual Wolves

Wolf - the Everybody's Erotic Dream
www.wolf.com/
Are you hot for wolves?
Wolf

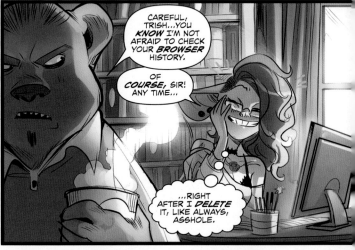

CAREFUL, TRISH...YOU *KNOW* I'M NOT AFRAID TO CHECK YOUR *BROWSER* HISTORY.

OF *COURSE*, SIR! ANY TIME...

...RIGHT AFTER I *DELETE* IT, LIKE ALWAYS, ASSHOLE.

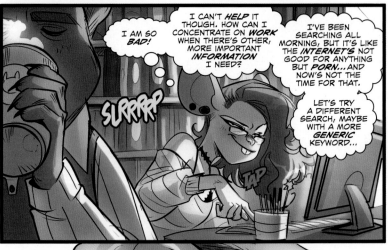

I AM SO *BAD!*

I CAN'T *HELP* IT THOUGH. HOW CAN I CONCENTRATE ON *WORK* WHEN THERE'S OTHER, MORE IMPORTANT *INFORMATION* I NEED?

I'VE BEEN SEARCHING ALL MORNING, BUT IT'S LIKE THE *INTERNET'S* NOT GOOD FOR ANYTHING BUT *PORN*...AND NOW'S NOT THE TIME FOR THAT.

LET'S TRY A DIFFERENT SEARCH, MAYBE WITH A MORE *GENERIC* KEYWORD...

SURRRRP

TAP

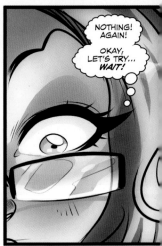

NOTHING! AGAIN!

OKAY, LET'S TRY... *WAIT!*

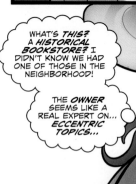

WHAT'S *THIS?* A *HISTORICAL BOOKSTORE?* I DIDN'T KNOW WE HAD ONE OF THOSE IN THE NEIGHBORHOOD!

THE *OWNER* SEEMS LIKE A REAL EXPERT ON... *ECCENTRIC* TOPICS...

SHE COULD HELP *ME*, HELP *LESLIE!* MAYBE *SHE* KNOWS WHAT THE INTERNET DOESN'T!

AND IF NOT...

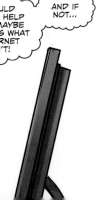

"MAYBE SHE'S GOT A BOOK THAT DOES!"
BOOOOKS
WOW... WHAT A WEIRD SHOP!
LIKE, I KNOW BOOKSTORES ARE GOING OUT OF BUSINESS AND STUFF. MAYBE THIS IS WHY...A CURTAIN INSTEAD OF A DOOR? STRANGE, MUCH?
COME ON, TRISH. IT'S COOL. REMEMBER... DO IT FOR LESLIE.
URGH!
AND I THOUGHT THE OUTSIDE WAS CREEPY!
THESE BOOKS ARE ALL SO OLD!
I DON'T EVEN KNOW WHERE TO START...
Q
R
S
CAN I HELP YOU WITH SOMETHING, MISS?

HEY UP THERE! MY NAME'S TRISH... ARE YOU SURE YOU DON'T NEED THE HELP?
YOU'RE PRETTY HIGH ON THAT LADDER...
OH, UP HERE? I'M FINE, TRISH.
I'M MISS... WEIGOLD. AND I'M TOTALLY AT HOME AMONG THESE STACKS...
I KNOW THE LOCATION OF EVERY BOOK WE HAVE HERE.
WHAT ARE YOU LOOKING FOR?
SOMETHING... FOR A FRIEND.
I'M LOOKING FOR ANYTHING ABOUT... STRANGE DREAMS.
WHAT TYPE OF STRANGE? EROTIC?
...YES. (HOW'D YOU KNOW THAT?) BUT ALSO...MAYBE JUST A LITTLE... AND I MEAN NOT SO MUCH, BUT A LITTLE... ILLEGAL?
YOUR FRIEND'S FANTASIZING ABOUT ANOTHER SPECIES, THEN?
YES! THAT'S A GOOD WAY TO SAY IT! THEY'RE NOT REALLY SLEEPING TOGETHER, BUT IN HER DREAMS?
SHE HAS HIM EVERY NIGHT.
WELL THEN...THIS MIGHT HELP YOU. AND ALSO THIS! AND THIS!
TELL ME...WHO ARE THE PLAYERS IN THIS ONEIRIC EROTICA? YOUR "FRIEND" AND WHOM ELSE?
STOP WITH THE TONE OF VOICE! WE'RE NOT TALKING ABOUT ME, I SWEAR! IT'S MY FRIEND LESLIE.
IT'S NOT ME...ANYWAY, IT'S LESLIE AND HER BIG BAD WOLF. SHE'S STILL HERSELF IN THE DREAM, BUT SHE'S WEARING A WEDDING DRESS.
A WHITE WOLF, BY CHANCE?
WHAT MORE CAN YOU TELL ME ABOUT YOUR FRIEND?
SHE'S A PIG...A LITTLE THICK, DEFINITELY...OH AND SHE HAS BLUE HAIR.
BLUE HAIR?
THAT'S STRANGE.
YEAH, I THINK IT'S SOME GENETIC DEFECT, BUT SHE ALWAYS SEEMED TO LIKE IT.
THAT'S JUST MADE ME THIN OF SOMETHING TRISH...
...FOLLO ME!

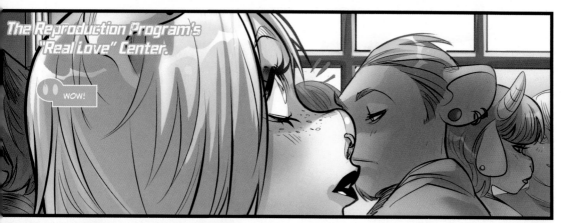

WOW!

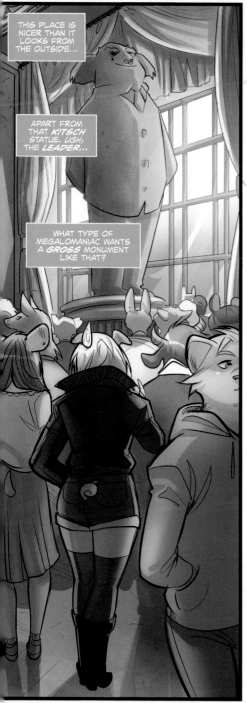

THIS PLACE IS NICER THAN IT LOOKS FROM THE OUTSIDE...

APART FROM THAT *KITSCH* STATUE. *UGH*, THE *LEADER*...

WHAT TYPE OF MEGALOMANIAC WANTS A *GROSS* MONUMENT LIKE THAT?

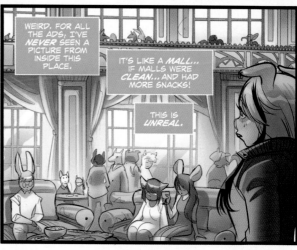

WEIRD. FOR ALL THE ADS, I'VE *NEVER* SEEN A PICTURE FROM INSIDE THIS PLACE.

IT'S LIKE A *MALL*... IF MALLS WERE *CLEAN*... AND HAD MORE SNACKS!

THIS IS *UNREAL*.

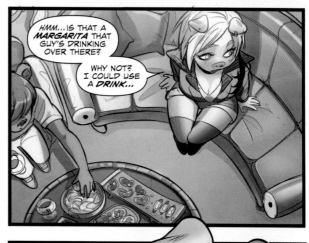

HMM...IS THAT A *MARGARITA* THAT GUY'S DRINKING OVER THERE?

WHY NOT? I COULD USE A *DRINK*...

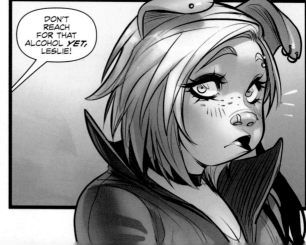

DON'T REACH FOR THAT ALCOHOL *YET*, LESLIE!

HI! I'M VIRGIL, YOUR SOCIAL ASSISTANT... BASICALLY YOUR CUPID!
I'LL BE YOUR GUIDE IN THIS NOBLE QUEST FOR A LIFEMATE!
NICE TO MEET YOU! DID YOU HEAR ME... TALKING TO MYSELF?
OF COURSE!
AH! SORRY!
SOMETIMES I THINK OUT LOUD... BUT ONLY WHEN I'M NERVOUS.
I'VE BEEN DOING IT SINCE I WAS A KID...IN FACT, THE KIDS USED TO MAKE FUN OF ME BECAUSE I ALWAYS TALKED TOO MUCH IN GENERAL...
L-LIKE I'M DOING NOW...
JUST RELAX, LES!
PAT PAT
IT'S COMPLETELY NORMAL TO BE A LITTLE NERVOUS. YOU'RE ABOUT TO GO THROUGH A BIG LIFE CHANGE! BUT DON'T WORRY, WE'LL BE HERE TO HELP YOU EVERY STEP OF THE WAY.
FIRST, WE COVER THE BASICS OF HOW THIS ALL HAPPENS HERE...
THEN I'LL GO OVER THE EVENING'S RULES, AND WE'LL MOVE YOU TO AN EXTERNAL FACILITY WHERE YOU'LL GET READY FOR THE FUN PART. NO SWEAT, I PROMISE!

Meanwhile, back to that mystery...
THANKS FOR THE TEA, IT SMELLS DELICIOUS.
IT'S A SECRET BREW MADE BY MY FAMILY. FLOWERS AND THREE SPECIAL KINDS OF APPLES.
IT IS GREAT...BUT WHAT ARE WE DOING BACK HERE?
THIS IS MY PRIVATE CORNER. THE BOOKS HERE ARE FROM MY PERSONAL COLLECTION.
SOMETHING YOU SAID EARLIER REMINDED ME OF ONE OF MY FAVORITE STORIES.
I DON'T THINK IT'S EXACTLY WHAT YOU'RE LOOKING FOR...BUT I WANTED TO SHOW IT TO YOU.
HERE! IT'S WORTH A LOOK, I THINK.
THIS?
I WAS EXPECTING SOMETHING MORE... ANTIQUE. SOME DUST MAYBE? MILDEW?
NOT EVERY GOOD BOOK'S AN OLD ONE, TRISH.
ONE OF MY REGULAR CUSTOMERS GOT IT FOR ME WHILE HE WAS TRAVELING ABROAD.
IT TELLS THE STORY OF A WONDERFUL, FORGOTTEN LAND.
THE BOOK IS VERY RARE, SINCE THESE DAYS, SOME OF ITS CONTENT IS CONSIDERED TO BE AGAINST NATURE...
UNNATURAL, SOME WOULD SAY.
THIS PART MIGHT INTEREST YOU, THOUGH.
LOOK AT THOSE TWO...DO YOU BELIEVE IN COINCIDENCE, TRISH?

HOLY--SHE LOOKS JUST LIKE LESLIE! HOW IS THAT POSSIBLE? THESE... THESE ARE JUST LEGENDS, RIGHT? FOLKTALES?
WELL, I GUESS SO...BUT EVERY LEGEND HAS TO START SOMEWHERE. WHY DON'T YOU HOLD ON TO THAT...
THANKS, I WILL! THIS IS UNBELIEVABLE... I'VE GOT A LOT TO THINK ABOUT.
THANK YOU AGAIN! I PROMISE I'LL RETURN IT AS SOON AS I CAN.
THAT'S A DEAL, MY DEAR... UNTIL THEN I'LL BE WAITING HERE WITH ANOTHER SPECIAL BREW.
Fulvius Gambots
TIJOUX
THE AUTHOR'S REALLY YOUNG IN THIS PHOTO, BUT LOOKING AT HIS BIRTHDATE...HE'S DEFINITELY OLD BY NOW. REALLY OLD. MAYBE THERE'S A WAY TO REACH OUT TO HIM, IF HE'S EVEN STILL ALIVE...
COME ON, SHERLOCK TRISH! THINK! YOU'VE FINALLY GOT A LEAD TO FOLLOW...
THIS ISN'T JUST A CURIOSITY ANYMORE...
"...THE STRANGE DREAMS OF LESLIE BLAIR ARE NOW A FULL-BLOWN ENIGMA!"
RealLove
SO, VIRGIL, WHERE ARE WE GOING NOW?

TO MAKE YOU EVEN MORE BEAUTIFUL THAN YOU ALREADY ARE, LESLIE!
IT DIDN'T TAKE LONG FOR THIS TO GET STRANGE... I HATE BEING IN THE SPOTLIGHT LIKE THIS.
HEY! YOU!
SOMETHING WRONG, OFFICER?
YOU'VE BEEN HANGING AROUND OUT HERE SINCE THAT NEW PIGLET ARRIVED. SOMETHING TELLS ME YOU TWO AREN'T FRIENDS.
SO WHAT ARE YOU, SOME KIND OF FUCKING STALKER? FATAL ATTRACTION TYPE?
YOU KNOW WHAT? DON'T ANSWER THAT.
WE'LL FIGURE IT OUT OURSELVES... LET'S SEE YOUR IDENTIFICATION, SICKO.
I'M SURE THIS IS JUST A MISUNDERSTANDING, OFFICERS...
THEN HELP US UNDERSTAND. YOU CAN START WITH YOU I.D.!
NOW!
I KNOW WHAT IT SOUNDS LIKE, BUT I HONESTLY FORGOT MY PAPERS TODAY. I DON'T KNOW HOW I COULD BE SO CARELESS...
RIGHT. LOOKS LIKE WE CAN FIGURE IT OUT TOGETHER DOWN AT THE STATION.
LET'S GO, HOODIE!

LET'S NOT!
SWAK
BAD MOVE, CREEP!
BZZZZZZ
BZZZZZZ
FUCK... I THINK HE BROKE MY JAW...
ASSAULTING AN OFFICER? THAT'S MORE THAN PROBABLE CAUSE, MORON. NOW WE GET TO SEARCH YOU...
WAIT, WHAT? WHAT THE HELL IS THIS? ARE YOU STALKING THAT PIG...
...OR HUNTING HER?

CHAPTER THREE

Then.
NO... NO!
CRASH
?
MOM WAS JOKING... SHE HAD TO BE...
S-SHE WASN'T SERIOUS--
OUCH! MY HAND!
IT HURTS!
LESLIE!
MOM?
WHATEVER YOU THINK YOU SAW... OR HEARD... I DON'T WANT TO KNOW.
BECAUSE YOU DIDN'T SEE IT, YOU HEAR ME?

YOU DON'T SAY A WORD OF THIS TO ANYONE, UNDERSTAND?
IF YOU DO... DADDY AND I COULD LOSE EVERYTHING. THE HOUSE, OUR JOBS...
EVEN YOU.
PROMISE ME YOU'LL KEEP QUIET, LESLIE... PROMISE ME!
OH-- OKAY, MOM...
"I PROMISE..."
MAYBE SHE IS A LITTLE... THICK. BUT APART FROM THAT, MISS LESLIE BLAIR IS PERFECTLY SUITABLE.
SO YOU SAY, DOCTOR. BUT WE'D STILL LIKE TO RUN THE USUAL TESTS.
WE CAN'T HAVE THE SPECIES GETTING WEAKER BECAUSE WE LET SOME BAD HEREDITY INTO THE MIX...
"WE'RE TRYING TO NATURALLY SELECT HERE!"
HMM... LOOKS LIKE SHE'S AVERAGE ON THE STRESS TEST.
ARE YOU MENSTRUATING REGULARLY?
ERR...
ARE YOU SEXUALLY ACTIVE? WHEN DID YOU LAST HAVE INTERCOURSE?
MEANING NATURAL INTERCOURSE, THAT IS. SAME-SPECIES? WE HAVE TO ASK.
I--
HOW HAVE YOUR BOWEL MOVEMENTS BEEN?

AAAAAH!
"HOW IS THAT RELEVANT?"
AAAH!
WHOA! YOU DIDN'T NEED TO GO THAT FAR! WELL, TOO LATE NOW, RIGHT?
STAY STILL, WOMAN!
HOW CAN I FIX THOSE HORRIBLE EYEBROWS IF YOU KEEP SQUIRMING?
GNNNH...
HMM... TOO CHASTE.
PLUS IT MAKES HER LOOK FAT.
NO... MAKES HER LOOK TOO EASY.
GUYS... CAN I SAY WHAT I THINK FOR A MINUTE?
NO! WE CAN'T WASTE TIME ON THAT!
COME ON! THERE'S STILL A TON OF DRESSES TO TRY ON.
AND WE HAVEN'T EVEN STARTED THE LINGERIE!
SIGH!
MAYBE WE LOSE THE PIERCINGS... SO AGGRESSIVE AND VULGAR.
AND THIS WEIRD HAIR... BLUE? WHAT'S THAT TRYING TO SAY?
KEEP THEM. IT'S GOOD.
WEIRD IS ALL THE RAGE THESE DAYS...
OKAY THEN, JUST A LITTLE MAKEUP...
...A BRUSH THROUGH THAT BLUE MESS...
AND WE'RE DONE!

FINALLY!
YOU'RE READY FOR YOUR POTENTIAL DREAM PARTNER... AND READY TO MATE!
YAY.
BUT...WHAT IF I DON'T LIKE HIM?
THEN I HOPE YOU'RE SECRETLY RICH AND ENJOY PAYING BIG-TIME TAXES!
...SO WHAT HAPPENS NOW?
NOW...WE WAIT! FOR YOUR DRIVER, I MEAN. HE SHOULD BE HERE...
OONK OONK
OH! THERE HE IS!
AND HE'S EARLY. THAT'S EVEN BETTER.
AND NOW, LESLIE...WE SAY GOODBYE.
BLAIR
GOOD LUCK WITH YOUR DATE! HOPEFULLY YOU'LL BE PLUMP WITH BABIES IN THE NEAR FUTURE. DON'T SWEAT IT, YOU LOOK GREAT!
T-THANKS. BYE, THEN.
"BYE"? MORE LIKE "FAREWELL," I'D SAY!
≷WHEW≶... I'D RATHER QUIT THAN SEE HER AGAIN.
NEVER SEEN SUCH AN INSUFFERABLE PIG...

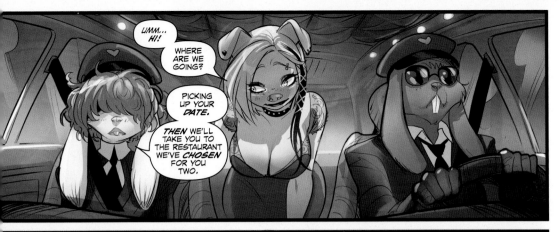

UMM... HI!

WHERE ARE WE GOING?

PICKING UP YOUR DATE.

THEN WE'LL TAKE YOU TO THE RESTAURANT WE'VE CHOSEN FOR YOU TWO.

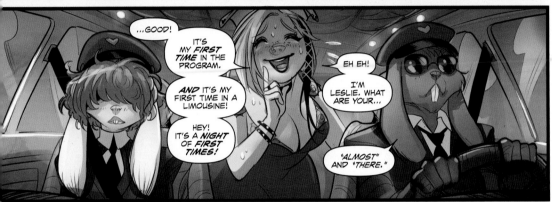

...GOOD!

IT'S MY FIRST TIME IN THE PROGRAM.

AND IT'S MY FIRST TIME IN A LIMOUSINE!

HEY! IT'S A NIGHT OF FIRST TIMES!

EH EH! I'M LESLIE. WHAT ARE YOUR...

"ALMOST" AND "THERE."

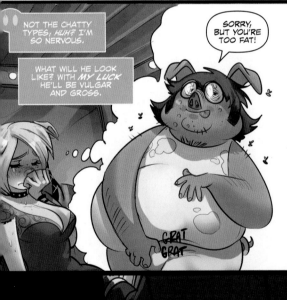

NOT THE CHATTY TYPES, HUH? I'M SO NERVOUS.

WHAT WILL HE LOOK LIKE? WITH MY LUCK HE'LL BE VULGAR AND GROSS.

SORRY, BUT YOU'RE TOO FAT!

GRAT GRAT

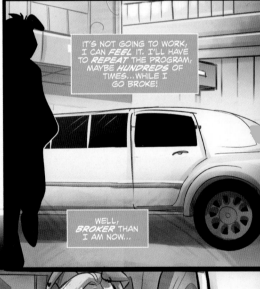

IT'S NOT GOING TO WORK, I CAN FEEL IT. I'LL HAVE TO REPEAT THE PROGRAM, MAYBE HUNDREDS OF TIMES...WHILE I GO BROKE!

WELL, BROKER THAN I AM NOW...

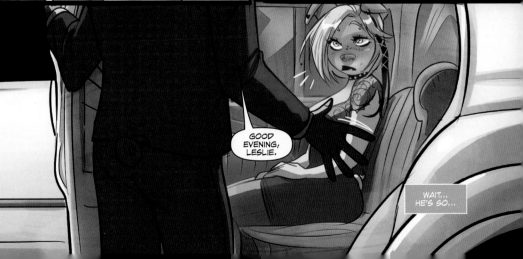

GOOD EVENING, LESLIE.

WAIT... HE'S SO...

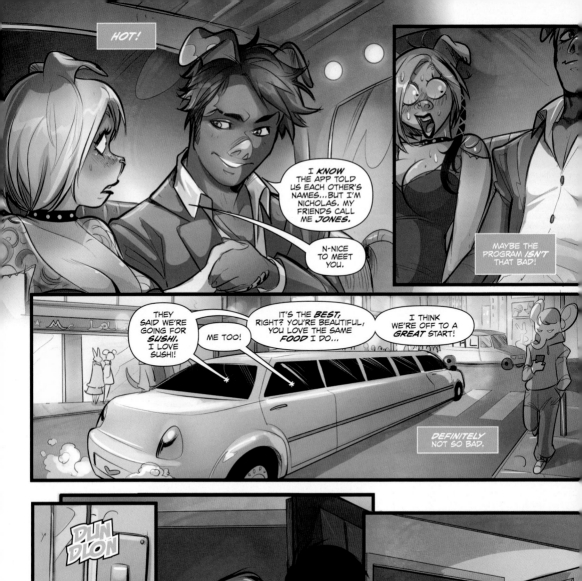

HOT!

I *KNOW* THE APP TOLD US EACH OTHER'S NAMES...BUT I'M NICHOLAS. MY FRIENDS CALL ME *JONES*.

N-NICE TO MEET YOU.

MAYBE THE PROGRAM *ISN'T* THAT BAD!

THEY SAID WE'RE GOING FOR *SUSHI*. I LOVE SUSHI!

ME TOO!

IT'S THE *BEST*, RIGHT? YOU'RE BEAUTIFUL, YOU LOVE THE SAME *FOOD* I DO...

I THINK WE'RE OFF TO A *GREAT* START!

DEFINITELY NOT SO BAD.

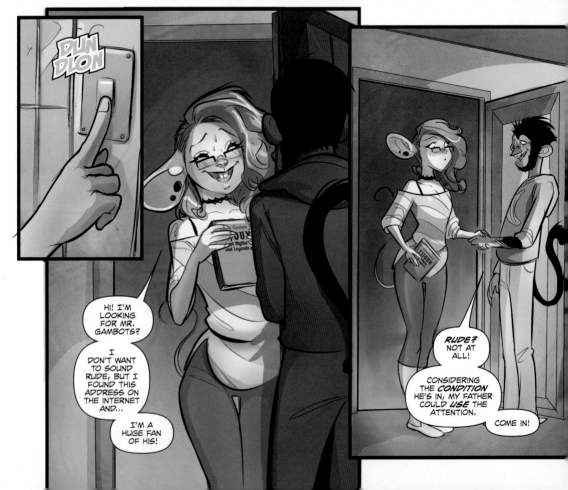

DUN DLON

HI! I'M LOOKING FOR MR. GAMBOTS?

I DON'T WANT TO SOUND RUDE, BUT I FOUND THIS ADDRESS ON THE INTERNET AND...

I'M A HUGE FAN OF HIS!

RUDE? NOT AT ALL!

CONSIDERING THE *CONDITION* HE'S IN, MY FATHER COULD *USE* THE ATTENTION.

COME IN!

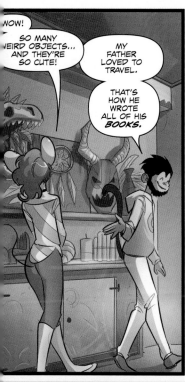

NOW!

SO MANY WEIRD OBJECTS... AND THEY'RE SO CUTE!

MY FATHER LOVED TO TRAVEL.

THAT'S HOW HE WROTE ALL OF HIS *BOOKS.*

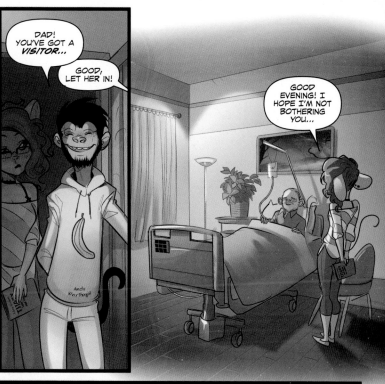

DAD! YOU'VE GOT A *VISITOR...*

GOOD, LET HER IN!

GOOD EVENING! I HOPE I'M NOT BOTHERING YOU...

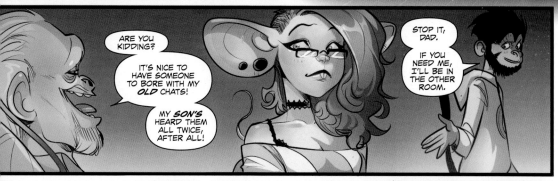

ARE YOU KIDDING?

IT'S NICE TO HAVE SOMEONE TO BORE WITH MY *OLD* CHATS!

MY *SON'S* HEARD THEM ALL TWICE, AFTER ALL!

STOP IT, DAD.

IF YOU NEED ME, I'LL BE IN THE OTHER ROOM.

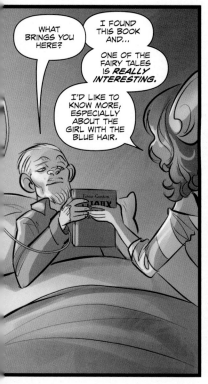

WHAT BRINGS YOU HERE?

I FOUND THIS BOOK AND...

ONE OF THE FAIRY TALES IS *REALLY INTERESTING.*

I'D LIKE TO KNOW MORE, ESPECIALLY ABOUT THE GIRL WITH THE BLUE HAIR.

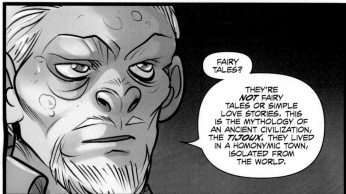

FAIRY TALES?

THEY'RE *NOT* FAIRY TALES OR SIMPLE LOVE STORIES. THIS IS THE MYTHOLOGY OF AN ANCIENT CIVILIZATION, THE *TIJOUX.* THEY LIVED IN A HOMONYMIC TOWN, ISOLATED FROM THE WORLD.

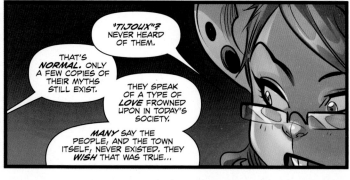

"TIJOUX"? NEVER HEARD OF THEM.

THAT'S *NORMAL.* ONLY A FEW COPIES OF THEIR MYTHS STILL EXIST.

THEY SPEAK OF A TYPE OF *LOVE* FROWNED UPON IN TODAY'S SOCIETY.

MANY SAY THE PEOPLE, AND THE TOWN ITSELF, NEVER EXISTED. THEY *WISH* THAT WAS TRUE...

BUT TIJOUX IS NOT FICTION! IT STILL EXISTS! IT'S ONE OF A KIND, UNKNOWN TO MOST TRAVELERS...BUT I SAW IT WITH MY OWN EYES! IT'S UNTOUCHED BY THE MODERN WORLD... EVERYONE THERE LIVES IN PEACE AND HARMONY.
SOME OF THEIR WOMEN ARE CONSIDERED TO BE BRIDES OF THE ANCIENT SPIRITS THEY BELIEVE PROTECT THEIR LAND. YOU ASKED ABOUT BLUE HAIR?
THE PROTAGONIST OF MY BOOK IS ONE OF THOSE BRIDES! BES!
Fulvius Gambots
TIJOUX
and Leg
THAT BOX SHOULD HAVE MY NOTES AND RESEARCH.
TAKE THEM, PLEASE.
...REALLY?
ABSOLUTELY. IT'S NOT LIKE I'LL BE AROUND TO USE THEM SOON. THEY'LL ONLY COLLECT DUST WHEN I'M GONE.
NO ONE HAS EVER BELIEVED MY STORIES, NOT EVEN MY SON. NO ONE...
...EXCEPT YOU.
LOOK...I KNOW YOU'RE NOT A FAN. NOT REALLY. I DON'T HAVE ANY OF THOSE LEFT.
PEOPLE THINK I'M SOME OLD CONSPIRACY THEORIST. MISSING TIME, FLAT EARTH, THAT TYPE OF STUFF...BUT THIS HAS ALWAYS BEEN REAL.
I DON'T KNOW WHY YOU'RE REALLY HERE, BUT I'M JUST HAPPY SOMEONE'S INTERESTED AT ALL. I DIDN'T THINK I'D LIVE LONG ENOUGH TO SEE IT.
TIJOUX
Lost Myths and Legends

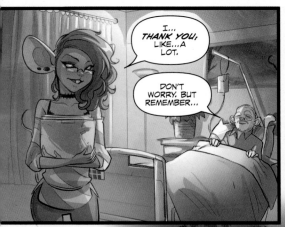

I... *THANK YOU*, LIKE...A LOT.

DON'T WORRY. BUT REMEMBER...

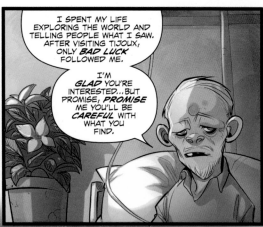

I SPENT MY LIFE EXPLORING THE WORLD AND TELLING PEOPLE WHAT I SAW. AFTER VISITING TIJOUX, ONLY *BAD LUCK* FOLLOWED ME.

I'M *GLAD* YOU'RE INTERESTED...BUT PROMISE, *PROMISE* ME YOU'LL BE *CAREFUL* WITH WHAT YOU FIND.

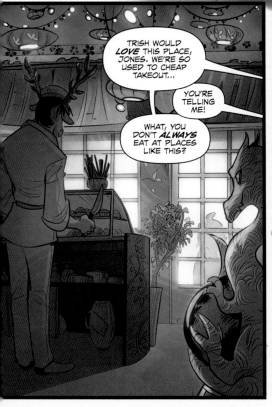

THANKS, I WILL.

ANYWAY...I'M NOT SEEKING ANSWERS FOR MYSELF.

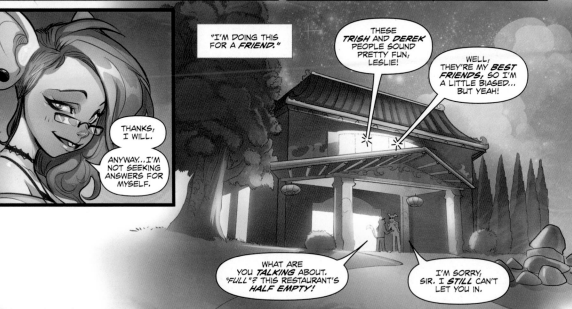

"I'M DOING THIS FOR A *FRIEND*."

THESE *TRISH* AND *DEREK* PEOPLE SOUND PRETTY FUN, LESLIE!

WELL, THEY'RE MY *BEST FRIENDS*, SO I'M A LITTLE BIASED... BUT YEAH!

WHAT ARE YOU *TALKING* ABOUT, *"FULL"?* THIS RESTAURANT'S *HALF EMPTY!*

I'M SORRY, SIR. I *STILL* CAN'T LET YOU IN.

TRISH WOULD *LOVE* THIS PLACE, JONES. WE'RE SO USED TO CHEAP TAKEOUT...

YOU'RE TELLING ME!

WHAT, YOU DON'T *ALWAYS* EAT AT PLACES LIKE THIS?

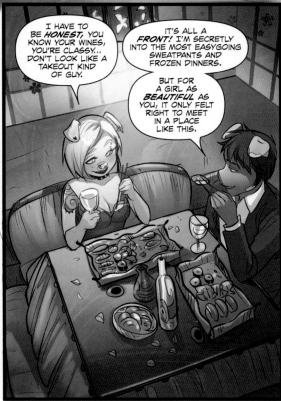

I HAVE TO BE *HONEST*, YOU KNOW YOUR WINES, YOU'RE CLASSY... DON'T LOOK LIKE A TAKEOUT KIND OF GUY.

IT'S ALL A *FRONT!* I'M SECRETLY INTO THE MOST EASYGOING SWEATPANTS AND FROZEN DINNERS.

BUT FOR A GIRL AS *BEAUTIFUL* AS YOU, IT ONLY FELT RIGHT TO MEET IN A PLACE LIKE THIS.

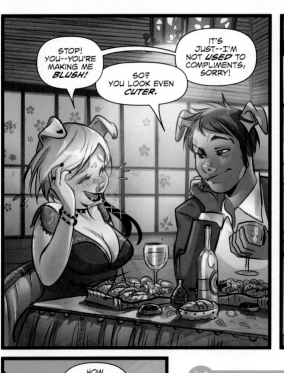

STOP! YOU--YOU'RE MAKING ME *BLUSH!*

SO? YOU LOOK EVEN *CUTER.*

IT'S JUST--I'M NOT *USED* TO COMPLIMENTS, SORRY!

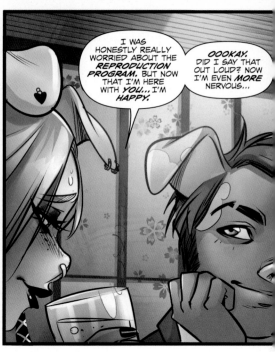

I WAS HONESTLY REALLY WORRIED ABOUT THE *REPRODUCTION PROGRAM.* BUT NOW THAT I'M HERE WITH *YOU...* I'M *HAPPY.*

OOOKAY. DID I SAY THAT OUT LOUD? NOW I'M EVEN *MORE* NERVOUS...

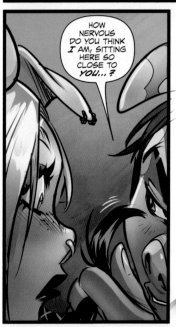

HOW NERVOUS DO YOU THINK *I* AM, SITTING HERE SO CLOSE TO *YOU...* ?

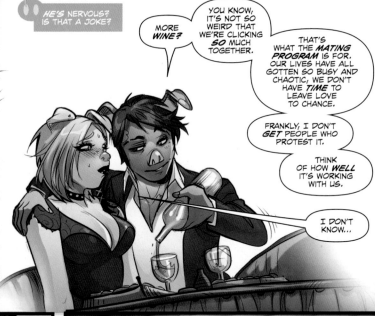

HE'S NERVOUS? IS THAT A JOKE?

MORE *WINE?*

YOU KNOW, IT'S NOT SO WEIRD THAT WE'RE CLICKING *SO* MUCH TOGETHER.

THAT'S WHAT THE *MATING PROGRAM* IS FOR. OUR LIVES HAVE ALL GOTTEN SO BUSY AND CHAOTIC, WE DON'T HAVE *TIME* TO LEAVE LOVE TO CHANCE.

FRANKLY, I DON'T *GET* PEOPLE WHO PROTEST IT.

THINK OF HOW *WELL* IT'S WORKING WITH US.

I DON'T KNOW...

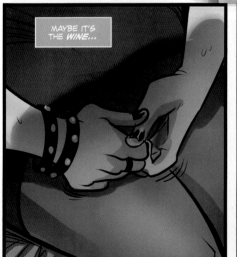

MAYBE IT'S THE *WINE...*

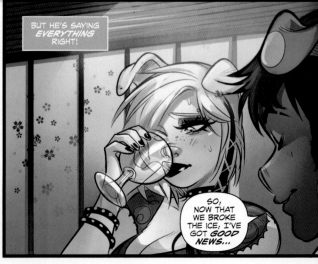

BUT HE'S SAYING *EVERYTHING* RIGHT!

SO, NOW THAT WE BROKE THE ICE, I'VE GOT *GOOD* NEWS...

YOU CAN HAVE ONE OF MY MAKI! GO AHEAD!
I WON'T ARGUE!
YUP, THAT'S IT. I ALREADY LOVE HIM.
I'LL HAVE TH--
TAC
NO, NO!
THE BON TON SAYS THAT IF YOU TAKE SOMETHING FROM SOMEONE ELSE'S PLATE, YOU HAVE TO TURN YOUR STICKS AROUND OR USE YOUR HANDS.
WANT ME TO HELP?
OK, THANKS.
TAKEOUT AND EASYGOING, MR. BON TON?
OKAY, I LIED...
I HAVE EXTREMELY SOPHISTICATED TASTES.
THAT'S WHY...
YOU DRIVE ME CRAZY.
AM I DREAMING?

IF THIS IS A DREAM, THERE SHOULD BE A WOLF. BUT HE'S NOT IN THE PROGRAM. HE NEVER COULD BE. HE'S JUST A FANTASY.
JONES SAID THE SAME THING: LOVE IS A THING THAT'S PROGRAMMED. I HAVE TO DO WHAT'S NORMAL FOR MY SPECIES...BUT FEELINGS ARE THE MOST NORMAL THINGS IN THE WORLD, RIGHT?
I FEEL LOVED IN MY DREAMS. MY HEART BEATS SO FAST JUST THINKING ABOUT THEM...MAYBE THERE'S NOTHING WRONG WITH THAT...
WAIT, WHAT AM I THINKING? AM I CRAZY?
JONES IS ONE OF MY SPECIES! HE'S CUTE, HE LIKES ME AND...HE'S RIGHT HERE! HE'S REAL!
S-SORRY.
MAYBE WE'RE GOING A LITTLE TOO FAST.
WHAT'S WRONG WITH ME?
I DIDN'T MEAN TO MOVE FAST...I JUST COULDN'T RESIST. I'M SORRY...
I'M SO STUPID!

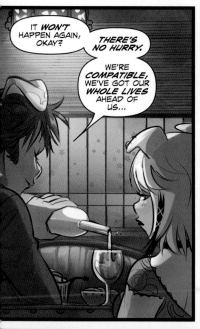
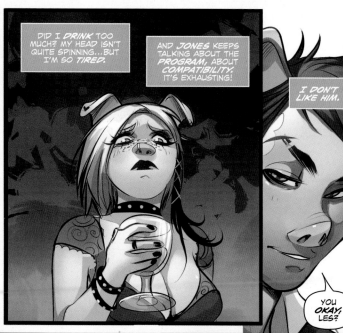

IT *WON'T* HAPPEN AGAIN, OKAY?

THERE'S NO HURRY.

WE'RE *COMPATIBLE*, WE'VE GOT OUR *WHOLE LIVES* AHEAD OF US...

DID I *DRINK* TOO MUCH? MY HEAD ISN'T QUITE SPINNING...BUT I'M SO *TIRED*.

AND *JONES* KEEPS TALKING ABOUT THE *PROGRAM*, ABOUT *COMPATIBILITY*. IT'S EXHAUSTING!

I DON'T LIKE HIM.

YOU *OKAY*, LES?

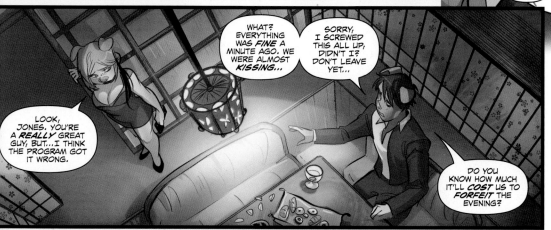

WHAT? EVERYTHING WAS *FINE* A MINUTE AGO. WE WERE ALMOST *KISSING*...

SORRY, I SCREWED THIS ALL UP, DIDN'T I? DON'T LEAVE YET...

LOOK, JONES. YOU'RE A *REALLY* GREAT GUY, BUT...I THINK THE PROGRAM GOT IT WRONG.

DO YOU KNOW HOW MUCH IT'LL *COST* US TO *FORFEIT* THE EVENING?

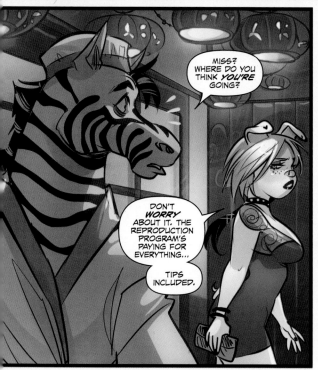

MISS? WHERE DO YOU THINK *YOU'RE* GOING?

DON'T *WORRY* ABOUT IT. THE REPRODUCTION PROGRAM'S PAYING FOR EVERYTHING...

TIPS INCLUDED.

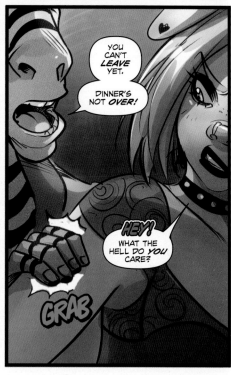

YOU CAN'T *LEAVE* YET.

DINNER'S NOT *OVER!*

HEY! WHAT THE HELL DO *YOU* CARE?

GRAB

WHAT ARE YOU DOING?
LET GO OF ME!
STAK
WAIT!
JUST WAIT, LES... WE CAN STILL FIX THIS. WE CAN FIX EVERYTHING.
WHAT'S HAPPENING?
EVERYONE'S LOOKING AT ME!
...JONES?!
CLOSE ALL THE EXITS NOW!
I WANT HER ROUNDED UP FOR THE SANCTUARY!

IT'S...IT'S A JOKE, RIGHT?
DEREK AND TRISH ARE GOING TO POP OUT AND SAY THEY REALLY GOT ME THIS TIME.
ANY SECOND NOW...
SHE WENT THAT WAY!
SPLIT UP!
YOU KNOW WHAT HAPPENS IF WE MAKE THE GLANCE WAIT.
TONIGHT IS THE NIGHT.
FAILURE IS NOT AN OPTION! NOT AFTER EVERYTHING WE'VE DONE TO INFILTRATE THE PROGRAM.

I DON'T KNOW WHAT'S GOING ON BUT I CAN WORRY ABOUT THAT LATER.
IF I CAN MAKE THE *WINDOW*, I'M *FREE!*
NO! IT *CAN'T* BE STUCK! COME ON...*OPEN!*
YOU'VE *GOT* TO OPEN!
?
WAIT, SOMETHING'S *HAPPENING.* SUDDENLY...
I DON'T *FEEL* SO WELL...

WHERE AM I?
THE ALBINO HAS SLEPT FOR TOO LONG... TRAPPED FOR CENTURIES.
WHO ARE THESE PEOPLE?
MH...
THE TIME HAS COME FOR HIM TO JOIN HIS BRIDE. SOON, BOTH OF THEM WILL BE AS ONE AS THEY AWAIT THE FULL AWAKENING OF HIS POWER!
WAIT, GLANCE! SHE'S STIRRING! STOP THE CEREMONY!
UH...
THE PIG GIRL WASN'T PROPERLY SEDATED, MAYBE WE SHOULD--
WE'VE ALREADY WAITED LONG ENOUGH.
NO!
THE CHOSEN GIRL WILL ONLY BE 25 ONCE! WE DON'T HAVE A CHOICE!

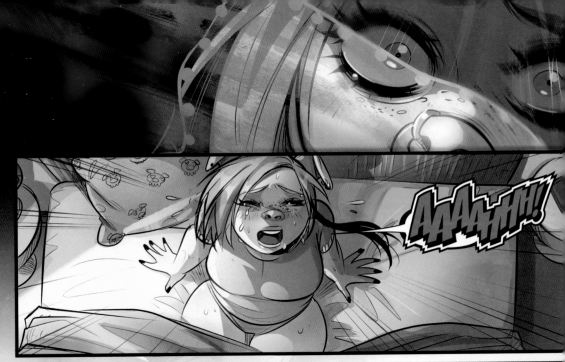

AAAAHHH!

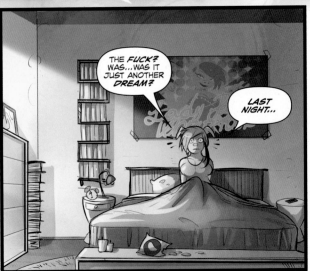

THE *FUCK?* WAS...WAS IT JUST ANOTHER *DREAM?*

LAST NIGHT...

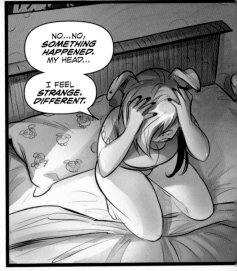

NO...NO, *SOMETHING HAPPENED.* MY HEAD...

I FEEL *STRANGE. DIFFERENT.*

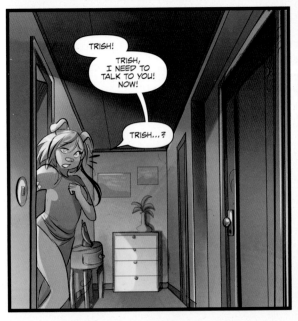

TRISH!

TRISH, I NEED TO TALK TO YOU! NOW!

TRISH...?

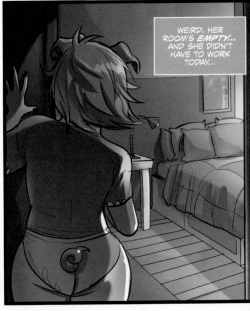

WEIRD. HER ROOM'S *EMPTY...* AND SHE DIDN'T HAVE TO WORK TODAY...

DEREK? IS TRISH WITH YOU? SHE WON'T ANSWER HER PHONE!
CALM DOWN, LES. ARE YOU OKAY?
I THINK... NO. I'M NOT OKAY, DEREK. CAN YOU COME OVER? I NEED HELP.
WHAT?! WHAT HAPPENED LAST NIGHT?
I KNOW IT SOUNDS CRAZY, BUT MY SHADOW FEELS HEAVY, LIKE A ROCK.
I FEEL SICK.
I'LL BE RIGHT THERE, JUST STAY CALM. WHATEVER HAPPENED, WE'LL FIGURE IT OUT. IT'S GOING TO BE OKAY!
"OKAY, DEREK...JUST HURRY."
DUN DLON DUN DLON
FINALLY!
LES!
DEREK! YOU DON'T KNOW HOW GOOD IT IS TO SEE YOU AND...
...ARE YOU SHITTING ME?
I'M SORRY, LES...

THEY WERE ALREADY OUTSIDE.
LESLIE BLAIR. YOU'RE IN A LOT OF TROUBLE. WE'RE GOING TO HAVE TO ASK YOU TO COME WITH US.
WHAT? WHY, OFFICER?
WE TALKED TO VIRGIL. DID YOU THINK YOUR SOCIAL ASSISTANT WOULDN'T KNOW YOU VANISHED FROM THE PERFECT DATE HE PREPARED FOR YOU?
YOU SKIPPED OUT ON THE DATE. NOW YOU CAN PAY THE FINE OR DEAL WITH THE SUMMONS.
NO! THAT'S NOT POSSIBLE, I WENT TO THE DATE!
THIS ISN'T RIGHT. THIS IS ALL A MISUNDERSTANDING, OFFICER...
EXACTLY.
A "MISUNDERSTANDING."
THAT'S EXACTLY WHY WE'RE HERE.
IF YOU WEREN'T AT YOUR DATE LAST NIGHT, MISS BLAIR, THEN WHERE WERE YOU BETWEEN 7:00 AND 11:00 PM?
WHERE WERE YOU WHEN YOUR ROOMMATE, TRISH FRIHA, WAS MURDERED?

CHAPTER
FOUR

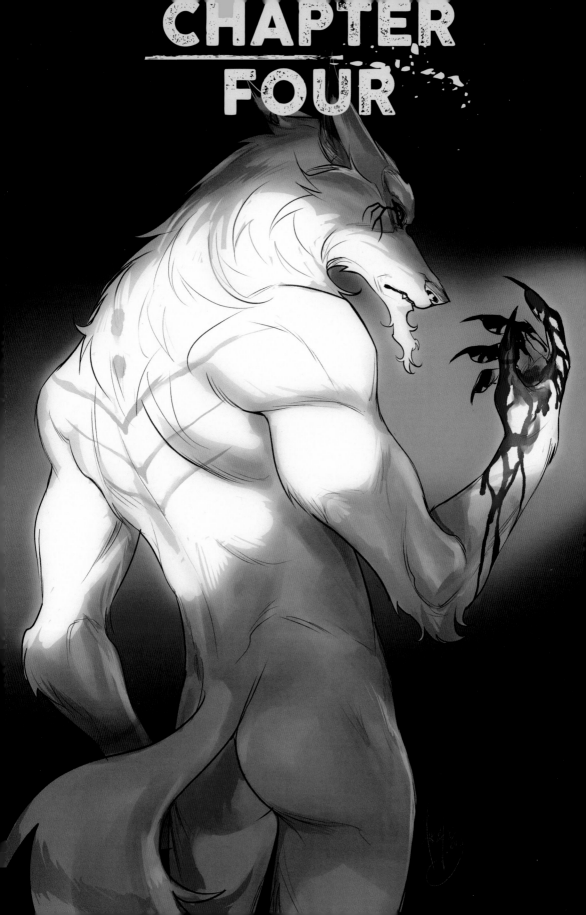

Then.
I SWEAR!
I JUST SAW JEN MAKING OUT WITH THAT GUY FROM CRIMINAL LAW!
AREN'T THEY... DIFFERENT SPECIES?
THAT'S THE POINT!
I DON'T WANT TO JUDGE... BUT DO YOU THINK SHE'S LIKE, CONTAGIOUS NOW?
IF ANYTHING I'D WORRY ABOUT YOUR IDIOCY SPREADING...
HEY!
TUMP
SORRY! I DIDN'T MEAN TO BUMP INTO YOU...
EASY, BLAIR.
HOW WEIRD IS SHE?
AND WHAT'S WITH THE MANNISH NAME? "LESLIE"?
IT'S ALSO A FEMALE NAME, SHEILA.
SHE'S STILL WEIRD.
AND THAT ATTITUDE OF HERS...
I HEARD HER FATHER JUST DIED. ISN'T SHE IN ONE OF YOUR CLASSES, TRISH?
YEAH.
I BET IT'S NOT LONG BEFORE THE SCHOOL KICKS HER OUT. I HEARD THE ONLY THING SHE'S GOING TO INHERIT IS DEBT.
NOT MUCH OF A LOSS. WHO'D MISS SOME BLUE-HAIRED PIG?

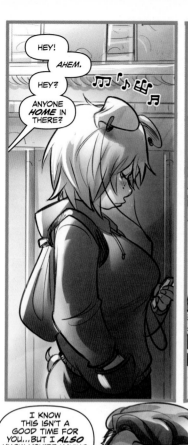

HEY!

AHEM.

HEY?

ANYONE *HOME* IN THERE?

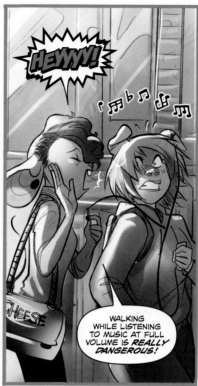

HEYYYY!

WALKING WHILE LISTENING TO MUSIC AT FULL VOLUME IS *REALLY DANGEROUS!*

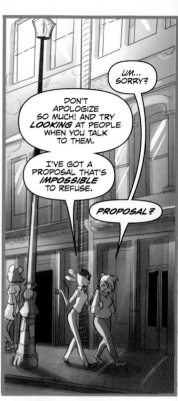

UM... SORRY?

DON'T APOLOGIZE SO MUCH! AND TRY *LOOKING* AT PEOPLE WHEN YOU TALK TO THEM.

I'VE GOT A PROPOSAL THAT'S *IMPOSSIBLE* TO REFUSE.

PROPOSAL?

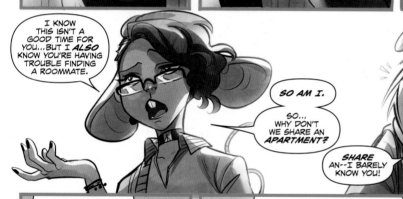

I KNOW THIS ISN'T A GOOD TIME FOR YOU...BUT I *ALSO* KNOW YOU'RE HAVING TROUBLE FINDING A ROOMMATE.

SO AM I.

SO... WHY DON'T WE SHARE AN *APARTMENT?*

SHARE AN--I BARELY KNOW YOU!

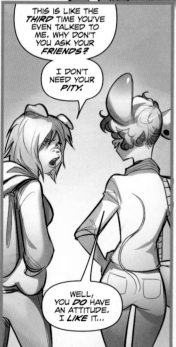

THIS IS LIKE THE *THIRD* TIME YOU'VE EVEN TALKED TO ME. WHY DON'T YOU ASK YOUR *FRIENDS?*

I DON'T NEED YOUR *PITY.*

WELL, YOU *DO* HAVE AN ATTITUDE. I *LIKE* IT...

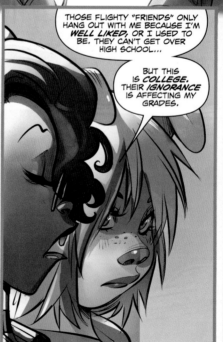

THOSE FLIGHTY "FRIENDS" ONLY HANG OUT WITH ME BECAUSE I'M *WELL LIKED,* OR I USED TO BE. THEY CAN'T GET OVER HIGH SCHOOL...

BUT THIS IS *COLLEGE.* THEIR *IGNORANCE* IS AFFECTING MY GRADES.

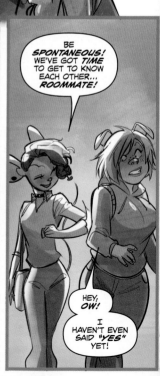

BE *SPONTANEOUS!* WE'VE GOT *TIME* TO GET TO KNOW EACH OTHER... *ROOMMATE!*

HEY, *OW!*

I HAVEN'T EVEN SAID *"YES"* YET!

WHAT WERE YOU LISTENING TO?
LADY PEG!
REALLY? I LOVE HER!
ACTUALLY... YOUR LOOK SORT OF REMINDS ME OF HER.
GET OUT...
I SWEAR! THE ONLY THING YOU'RE MISSING'S BLACK LIPSTICK AND YOU'D BE A REAL ROCKER.
ARE YOU KIDDING?!
"YOU'RE SO FULL OF IT."
THIS IS YOUR FRIEND. LOOK AT THE STATE SHE'S IN.
THE CORONER SAYS SHE DIED BETWEEN 9:00 AND 11:00 LAST NIGHT... THE EXACT TIME YOU SHOULD'VE BEEN ON YOUR DATE.
MISS BLAIR...
BUT YOU WEREN'T ON IT.
IN FACT, NO ONE KNOWS WHERE YOU WERE LAST NIGHT. CARE TO ENLIGHTEN US?
I THOUGHT I WAS ON THE DATE! I'M-- I'M BEING FRAMED!
MY FRIEND DEREK DROPPED ME WITH THE SOCIAL ASSISTANT... AND THEN I WENT TO THE RESTAURANT!
ENOUGH! WE KNOW THAT'S NOT TRUE!
THAT PLACE HAS BEEN CLOSED FOR YEARS!
NOT TO MENTION THOSE RABBITS YOU MENTIONED AND WHOEVER IT WAS THAT TOLD YOU HE WAS THE REAL "JONES."
YOUR SOCIAL ASSISTANT HAS NO IDEA WHAT HAPPENED TO YOU AFTER YOU GOT IN THAT CAR.
NILES... WE'VE BEEN QUESTIONING HER FOR HOURS.
WE CAN'T HOLD HER. THERE ARE OTHER SUSPECTS... I THINK THIS IS IT, FOR THE MOMENT.
THERE'S NO ACTIONABLE EVIDENCE AGAINST YOU, MISS BLAIR... YOU'RE FREE TO GO.
FOR NOW.
DON'T LEAVE TOWN. OH, AND YOUR BELONGINGS HAVE BEEN CONFISCATED AS EVIDENCE... ENJOY.

"WE'LL BE *WATCHING* YOU, PIG."

MY *BABY!*

SNFF

SNFF

STAY *STRONG.* TRISH IS WITH *ANOTHER* MOTHER NOW, MOTHER NATURE...AND SHE WATCHES OVER *ALL* OF US.

SHE'S PART OF *EVERYTHING* NOW, JUST AS WE ALL ARE BEFORE OUR *BEING*... SHE'S ALL AROUND US.

ARE YOU SURE YOU DON'T WANT TO GET CLOSER?

NO, DEREK... WORD TRAVELS *FAST.* THEY ALL KNOW I'M A *SUSPECT.*

HERE IS FINE. IT'LL ONLY *HURT* THEM TO SEE ME, AND THEY'RE *ALREADY* SUFFERING ENOUGH.

AND I... I DIDN'T EVEN GET TO SAY *GOODBYE.*

IT'S *JUST* LIKE WITH MY *DAD.* EVERYONE I *LOVE* ENDS UP *DEAD...*

MAYBE YOU SHOULD LET ME *GO,* DEREK... PROBABLY *SAFER* THAT WAY.

I'LL ALWAYS BE WITH YOU, LES.
LET'S GO TO MY PLACE. THE COPS TOOK ALL YOUR STUFF, YOU CAN'T STAY IN THAT FLAT ANYMORE.
YOU'LL SEE...
"...EVERYTHING IS GOING TO BE OKAY."
EEEEE
EEEEEEE
EEEEEEEE

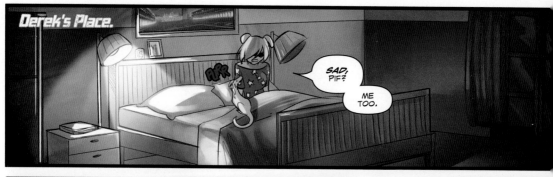

SAD, PIF?

ME TOO.

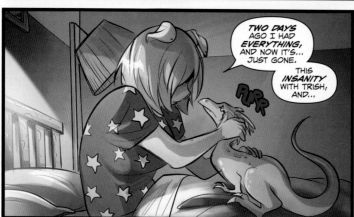

TWO DAYS AGO I HAD *EVERYTHING*, AND NOW IT'S... JUST GONE.

THIS *INSANITY* WITH TRISH, AND...

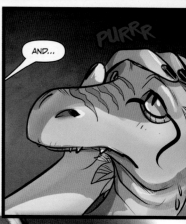

AND...

PURRR

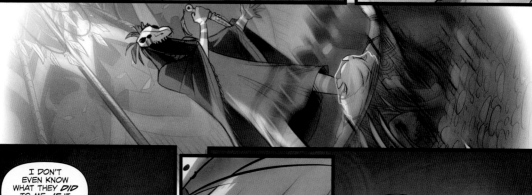

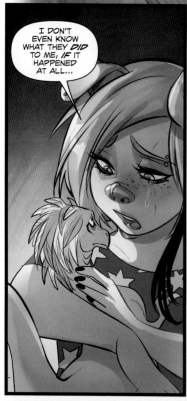

I DON'T EVEN KNOW WHAT THEY *DID* TO ME, *IF* IT HAPPENED AT ALL...

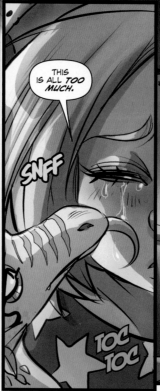

THIS IS ALL *TOO MUCH*.

SNFF

TOC TOC

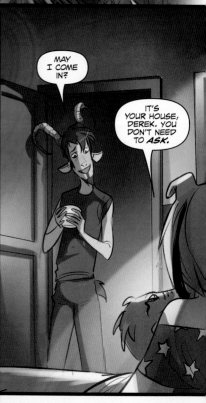

MAY I COME IN?

IT'S YOUR HOUSE, DEREK. YOU DON'T NEED TO *ASK*.

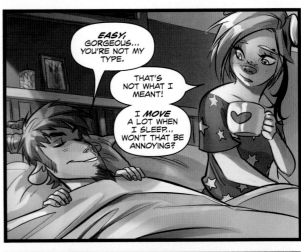

EASY, GORGEOUS... YOU'RE NOT MY TYPE.

THAT'S NOT WHAT I MEANT!

I MOVE A LOT WHEN I SLEEP... WON'T THAT BE ANNOYING?

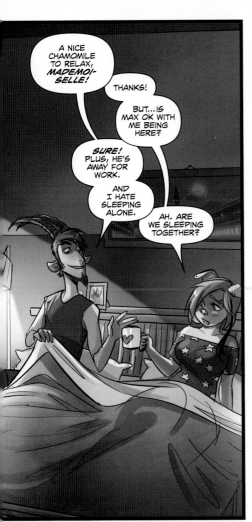

A NICE CHAMOMILE TO RELAX, MADEMOI-SELLE!

THANKS!

BUT...IS MAX OK WITH ME BEING HERE?

SURE! PLUS, HE'S AWAY FOR WORK.

AND I HATE SLEEPING ALONE.

AH. ARE WE SLEEPING TOGETHER?

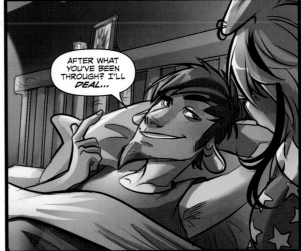

AFTER WHAT YOU'VE BEEN THROUGH? I'LL DEAL...

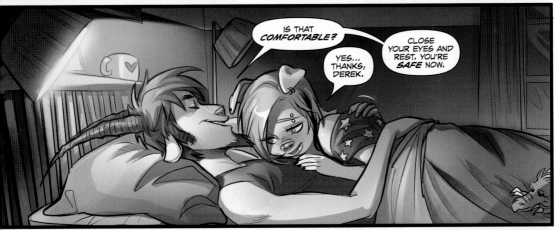

IS THAT COMFORTABLE?

YES... THANKS, DEREK.

CLOSE YOUR EYES AND REST. YOU'RE SAFE NOW.

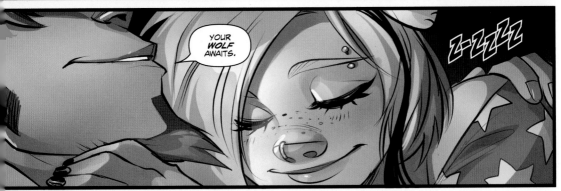

YOUR WOLF AWAITS.

Z-ZZZ

YES... I'M HAPPY NOW.
I WOULD STAY LIKE THIS FOREVER.
WITH THE WOLF OF MY DREAMS.
WAIT A MINUTE!
EVERYTHING IS DIFFERENT!
I CAN SEE EVERY DETAIL, HEAR MY OWN BREATH...
THIS ISN'T A DREAM...
IT'S A MEMORY.
BES...
ARE YOU SCARED?
NO, MY GROOM. I WAS BORN FOR THIS.
YOU'RE DIFFERENT FROM THE OTHER BRIDES...
IT WILL BE HARD TO LEAVE YOU.
DO WE REALLY HAVE TO DO IT?

I'M SORRY.
I WANT YOU SO MUCH...I NEED YOU...ALL TO MYSELF...
THAT'S WHY THIS HAS TO END.
SHUUKK

LES?!
GLLG KOFF KOFF
CRRNNH
AAAH!
TMP
YOU GOT ONE THING RIGHT...
I...
...AM NOT...
...LIKE THE OTHER BRIDES!
SLITCH

AAAAAAH!
YOU OKAY, LES?
AAAH!
D-DON'T TOUCH ME!
LESLIE, IT'S ME!
WHAT'S-- WHAT'S WRONG?
BLUARGH

TRISH WAS RIGHT!
THESE DREAMS AREN'T NORMAL!
THEY'RE MEMORIES, DEREK! MEMORIES FROM ANOTHER LIFE...
THAT'S-- THAT'S CRAZY! YOU'RE NOT THINKING STRAIGHT, LES.
COME ON...
...LET'S GET BACK TO BED.
A GOOD NIGHT'S SLEEP SHOULD SORT THIS OUT.
WE HAVE TO RUN! WE'RE IN DANGER!
N-NO... NO! NO!
YOU DON'T EXIST. WHY SHOULD I LISTEN TO YOU, MONSTER?
MONSTER? ME?
I DO EXIST! YOU BONDED ME TO YOUR SOUL SO MANY LIFETIMES AGO... ARE YOU NOT BEGINNING TO REMEMBER?
YOU MUST TRUST ME, THERE'S NO OTHER CHOICE.
OTHERWISE... WE BOTH DIE.

OKAY...
WHAT ARE YOU DOING?
I DON'T KNOW.
BUT WE HAVE TO RUN, DEREK. TRUST ME.
I WANT TO...BUT NO, LES. WE CAN'T JUST RUN OFF. I DON'T EVEN KNOW WHAT'S HAPPENING!
THIS DOESN'T MAKE ANY SENSE. YOU NEED TO CALM DOWN AND GO BACK TO BED.
YOU!
LET US PASS, TRAITOR!
UH?
I...
...
DEREK, THAT WASN'T ME...I'M SORRY...
I DIDN'T MEAN THAT. YOU-- YOU'RE THE ONLY ONE I CAN TRUST.

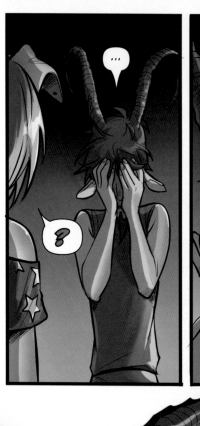
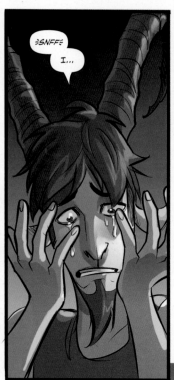
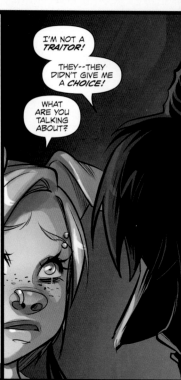

. . .

?

≥SNFF≥ I...

I'M NOT A TRAITOR!

THEY--THEY DIDN'T GIVE ME A CHOICE!

WHAT ARE YOU TALKING ABOUT?

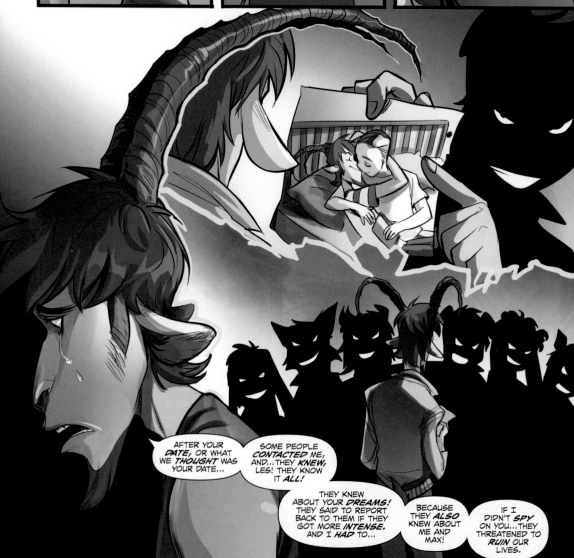

AFTER YOUR DATE, OR WHAT WE THOUGHT WAS YOUR DATE...

SOME PEOPLE CONTACTED ME, AND...THEY KNEW, LES! THEY KNOW IT ALL!

THEY KNEW ABOUT YOUR DREAMS! THEY SAID TO REPORT BACK TO THEM IF THEY GOT MORE INTENSE. AND I HAD TO...

BECAUSE THEY ALSO KNEW ABOUT ME AND MAX!

IF I DIDN'T SPY ON YOU...THEY THREATENED TO RUIN OUR LIVES.

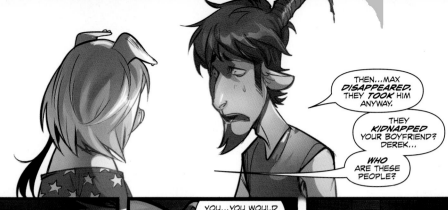

THEN...MAX *DISAPPEARED*. THEY *TOOK* HIM ANYWAY.

THEY *KIDNAPPED* YOUR BOYFRIEND? DEREK...

WHO ARE THESE PEOPLE?

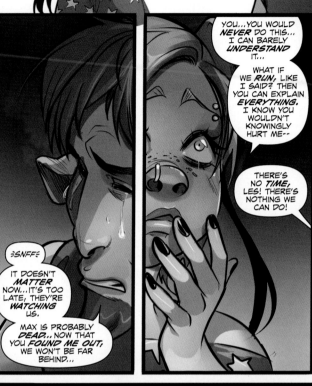

YOU...YOU WOULD *NEVER* DO THIS... I CAN BARELY *UNDERSTAND* IT...

WHAT IF WE *RUN*, LIKE I SAID? THEN YOU CAN EXPLAIN *EVERYTHING*. I KNOW YOU WOULDN'T KNOWINGLY HURT ME--

THERE'S NO *TIME*, LES! THERE'S NOTHING WE CAN DO!

⋛SNFF⋚ IT DOESN'T *MATTER* NOW...IT'S TOO LATE, THEY'RE *WATCHING* US.

MAX IS PROBABLY *DEAD*...NOW THAT YOU *FOUND ME OUT*, WE WON'T BE FAR BEHIND...

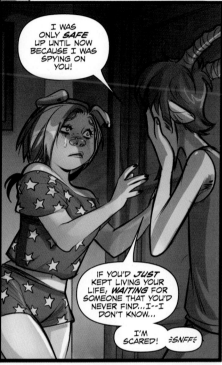

I WAS ONLY *SAFE* UP UNTIL NOW BECAUSE I WAS SPYING ON YOU!

IF YOU'D *JUST* KEPT LIVING YOUR LIFE, *WAITING* FOR SOMEONE THAT YOU'D NEVER FIND...I--I DON'T KNOW...

I'M SCARED! ⋛SNFF⋚

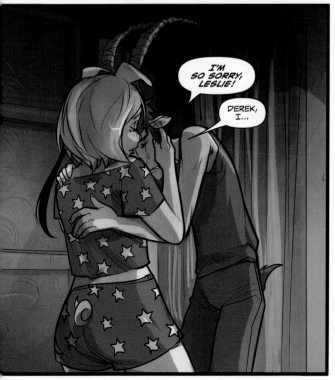

I'M SO SORRY, LESLIE!

DEREK, I...

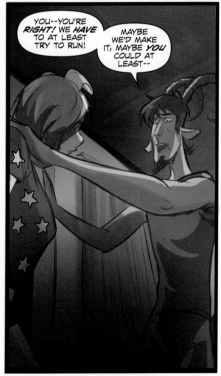

YOU--YOU'RE *RIGHT!* WE *HAVE* TO AT LEAST TRY TO RUN!

MAYBE WE'D MAKE IT, MAYBE *YOU* COULD AT LEAST--

BANG
THIS MIGHT SEEM SURPRISING, LESLIE, BUT IT SHOULDN'T BE.
YOUR FRIEND WAS A REAL LOSER. THE KIND THAT RUINS EVERYONE'S WELL-LAID PLANS.
THIS WAS ONLY EVER GOING TO END ONE WAY.
JONES?!
HE COULDN'T EVEN KEEP YOU IN CHECK. NOW LOOK, HERE I AM GETTING MY HANDS DIRTY...I HATE GETTING MY HANDS DIRTY.
AND YOU... YOU JUST COULDN' BEHAVE UNTIL THE AWAKENING, COULD YOU?

YOU--
YOU SHOT DEREK!
HE'S...HE'S DEAD, JUST LIKE TRISH. AND YOU...
WHY WON'T YOU JUST LEAVE ME ALONE?!
YOU'RE A CLEVER PIG, LESLIE...
YOU HAVE TO KNOW WE CAN'T DO THAT.
CRUNCH
BANG BANG
BANG
WAIT, YOU IDIOT!
THE GLANCE NEEDS HER ALIVE!
UGH! WHAT?
TUMP
...WHO ARE YOU?
YOU... I THINK THERE'S BEEN ENOUGH GAMES TODAY.

GOOD.
BECAUSE I'M NOT PLAYING!
SLATCH
SLATCH
BANG
!
CRACK
...WE NEED TO GO.
YOU-- YOU SAVED ME...
WHY?
I'M ON YOUR SIDE, LESLIE...
?
BUT YOU...

I'M ON YOUR SIDE, I SAID.
YOU'RE HIM!
KSSS
NO, I'M NOT. I WILL EXPLAIN EVERYTHING. BUT FOR NOW...
WE NEED TO GET OUT OF HERE!
NO!
LET ME GO!
YOU'RE-- YOU'RE THE WOLF IN MY DREAMS! HOW?!
I TOLD YOU! I'M NOT THAT BASTARD!
NOW COME ON!
AAAH!
BUT BEFORE WE GO...
CLIC
LET'S MAKE SURE THEY CAN'T SEE WHERE WE'RE HEADED.
FZZZZ

FZZZZ
FZZZZ
FZZZZ
WE'VE BEEN... INCAUTIOUS. SOMEONE IS CLEARLY WORKING AGAINST US.
BUT HOW? NO ONE SHOULD KNOW WHO WE ARE.
THAT WAS TERRIBLE!
YES, GLANCE. OUR AGENTS FAILED YOU. THEY WILL PAY.
NO...BRING JONES AND THOSE TRIGGER-HAPPY RABBITS TO ME. THERE'S MORE TO DO.
OUR NEXT STEP IS SIMPLE. LESLIE BLAIR WILL FIND NO SHELTER, NO PEACE. HER LIFE WILL BE A MAZE OF CONSTANT PANIC...
PUSHING HER DIRECTLY INTO OUR HANDS.

EXTRA
NATURAL

EXTRA

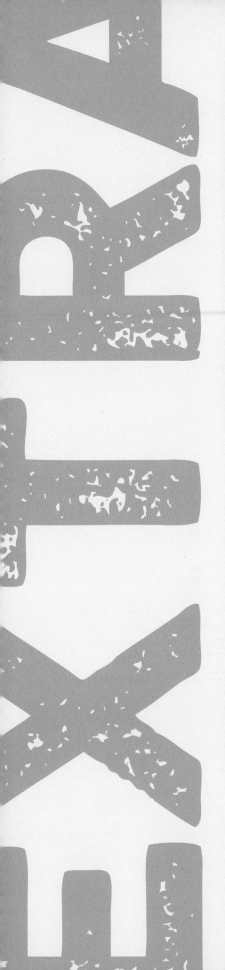

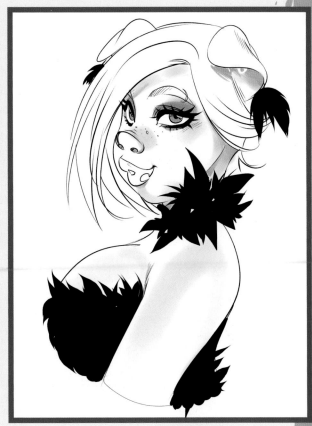

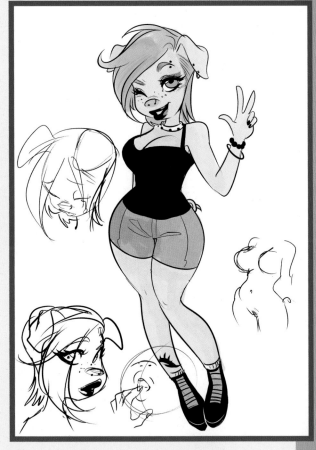

I ♥ PEPPA PIG

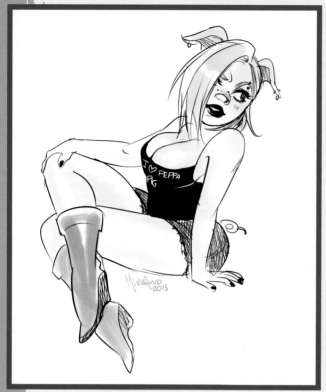

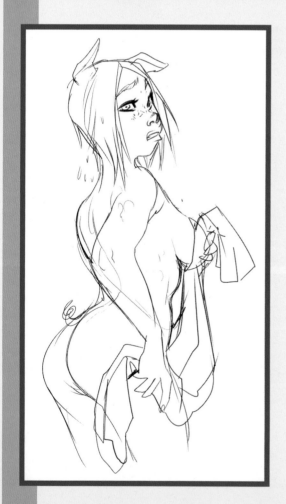

Miranda 2015

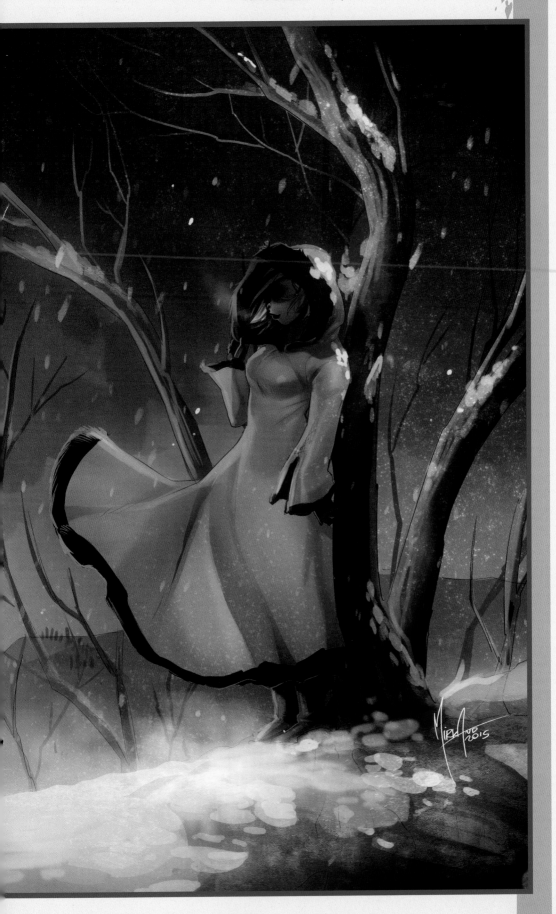

#LESLIEPIG
MirkAnd 16
SOY

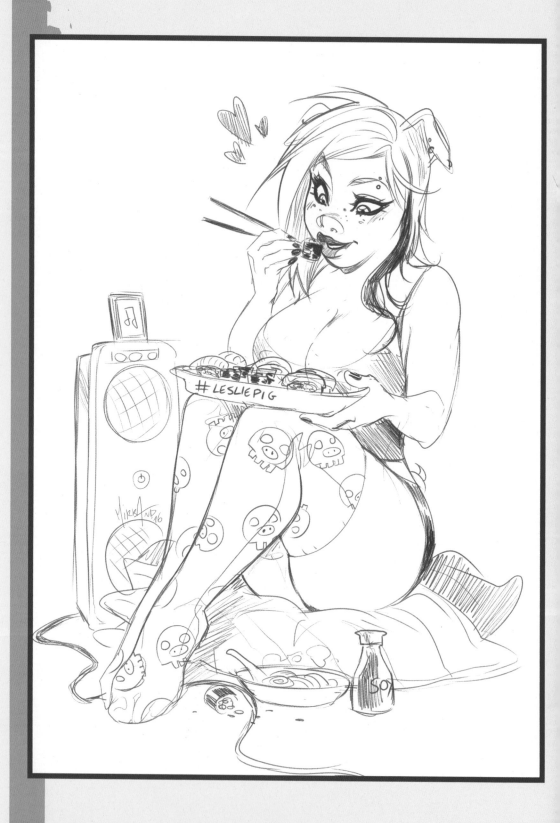

VARIANT
COVERS

MA
NA
RA

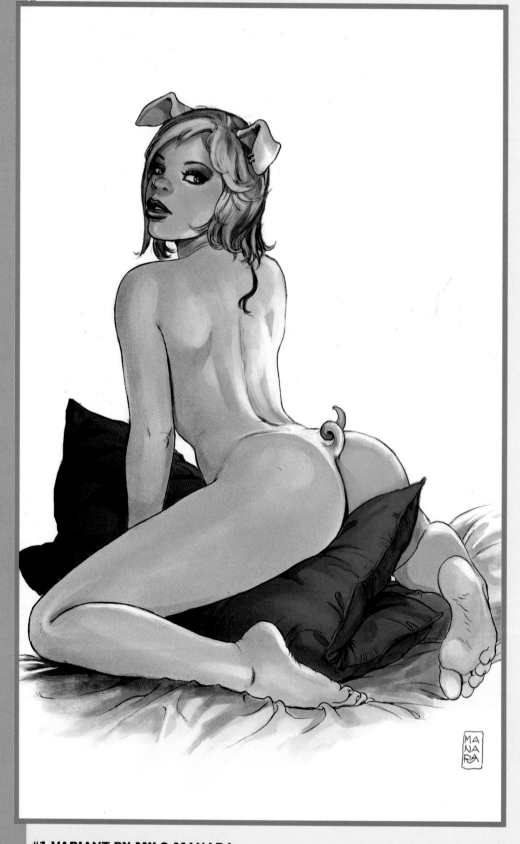

#1 VARIANT BY MILO MANARA

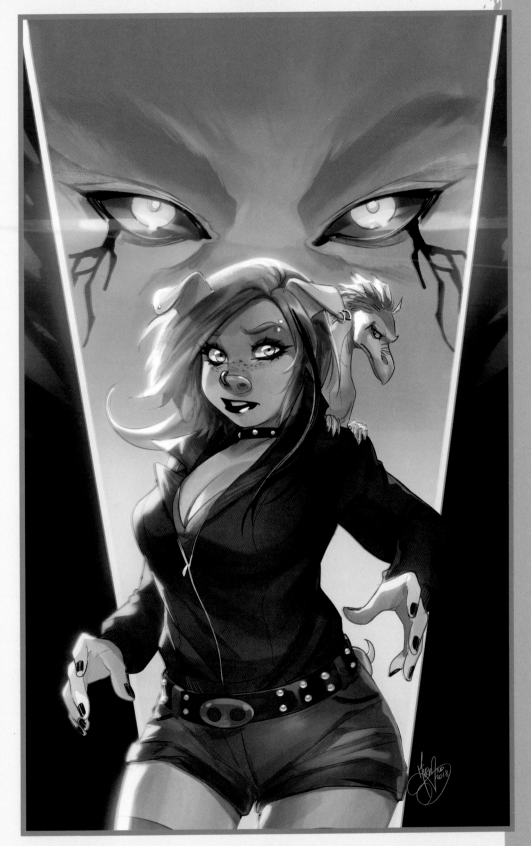

#1 SDCC VARIANT BY MIRKA ANDOLFO

#2 VARIANT BY ARTGERM

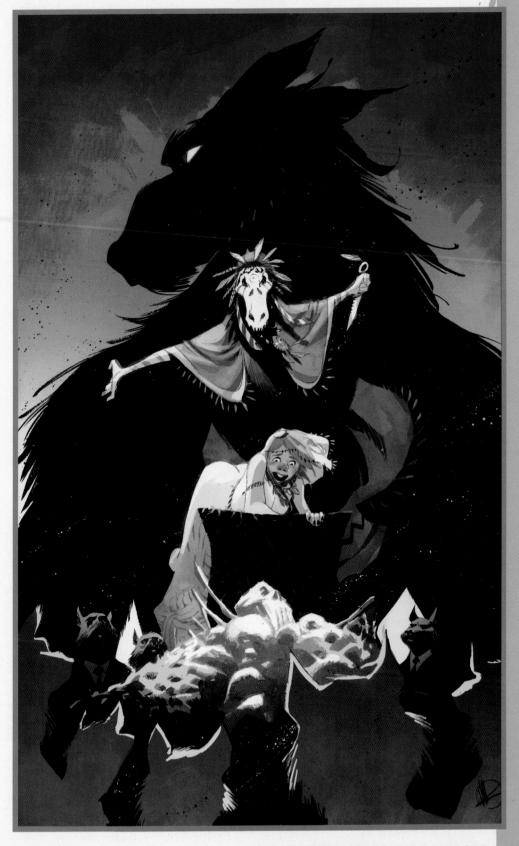

#3 VARIANT BY MATTEO SCALERA

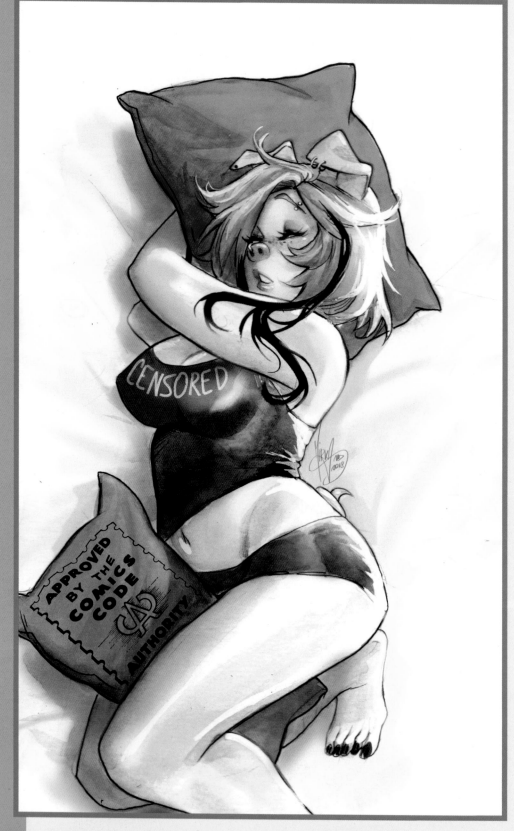

#3 COMICS CODE AUTHORITY VARIANT - CBLDF BY MIRKA ANDOLFO

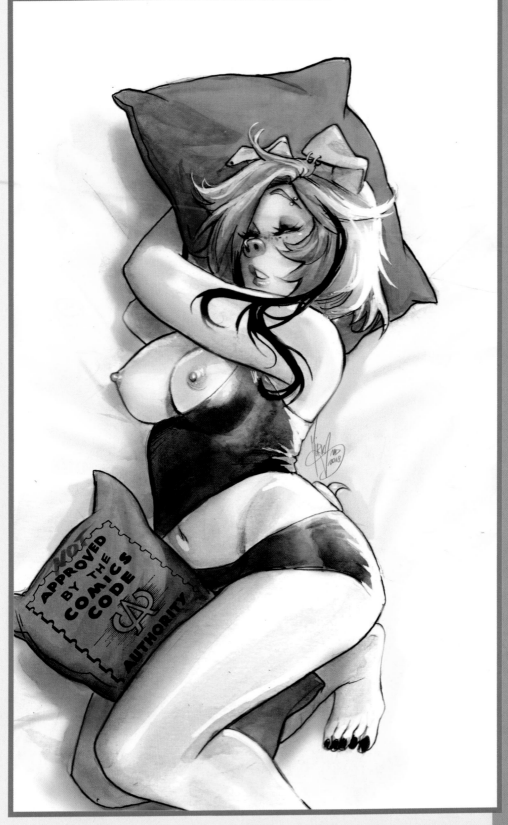

#3 COMICS CODE AUTHORITY NAKED VARIANT - CBLDF BY MIRKA ANDOLFO

B.

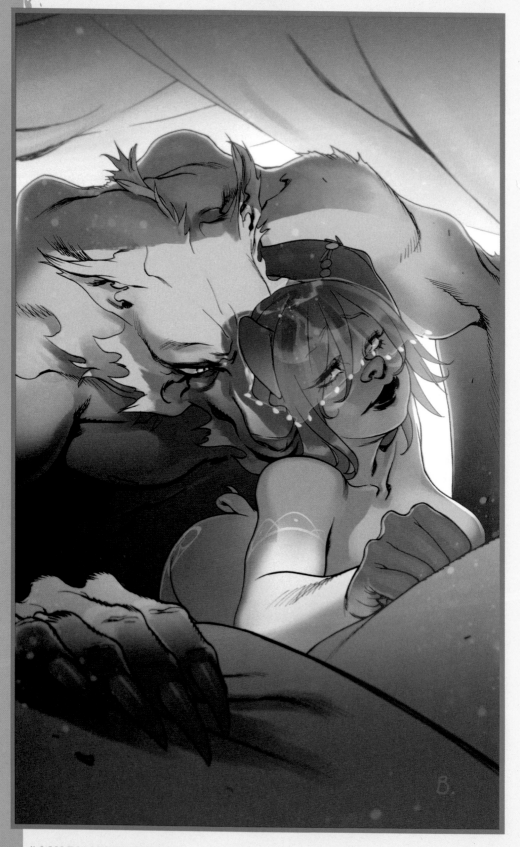

#4 VARIANT BY BENGAL

I put all of myself into Unnatural. I started working on it around three years ago, in my "free time," and I never expected what came next. Seeing Leslie and her companions speaking English now is incredibly emotional for me. This is why I can never thank Panini Comics enough, starting with Marco Lupoi and Sara Mattioli, for believing in it. The same goes for my editors, Diego Malara and Marco Ricompensa, who guided me step by step and helped me to avoid "getting lost." The guys at Arancia Studio, who took care of the packaging of the US edition—lettering (Fabio Amelia) and color assists (Gianluca Papi with flat colors by Simon Tessuto, Erika Migliore and Gabriella Sinopoli.) Without them, I could never have colored everything in time. Thank you!

Thanks to all the artists who made the variant covers, my friends, for helping me or just for supporting me with their friendship. Andrea Meloni and Steve Orlando: you're great, guys! And thanks to Davide, for everything. Obviously, thanks to Image Comics for having believed so strongly in my project, and to all the readers for the support. I cannot wait to tell you what else the poor Leslie will still have to endure...♥

MIRKA

Mirka Andolfo is an Italian creator, working as an artist at DC Comics (*Harley Quinn*, *Wonder Woman*, *DC Bombshells*) and Vertigo (*Hex Wives*). She has drawn comics at Marvel, Dynamite and Aspen Comics. As a creator, *Unnatural* (published so far in Italy, Germany, France, Spain, Poland, Mexico) is her second book, after *Sacro/Profano* (published in Italy, France, Belgium, Netherlands, Spain, Germany and Serbia). You can reach Mirka on her social media channels and on her website: *mirkand.eu*

f mirkand.works   **🐦** @Mirkand   **📷** @mirkand89